MW01114930

Grounded

Paranormal Penny Mysteries, Volume 1

Sarah Hualde

Published by Indie Christian Writers, 2020.

Copyright

Grounded
Copyright 2020 Sarah Hualde
Written by Sarah Hualde
ISBN: 1703378970

To Han Solo:

Because I love him and he knows.

Bonus

<u>Free Ebook- Penny Mystery 1.5</u>[1]

---

1. https://storyoriginapp.com/giveaways/be376e58-a177-11ec-9c75-036090dfe8b2

Supernatural Suspense meets Paranormal Mystery in the Penny Nicols Series. You'll cheer for Penny, her quirky cat, and their extra extraordinary friends.

Don't stop at Grounded. See what the winter holds for Penny. Download Frosted- Penny's seasonal short.
For FREE on Ebook
Visit the site below to snag your copy:
https://storyoriginapp.com/giveaways/be376e58-a177-11ec-9c75-036090dfe8b2

;) enjoy

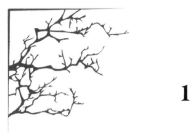

1

"I'M LOSING MY MIND!" I screamed into my pillow.

Why in the world was I about to talk on the phone to my stalker? I cringed at the question. Stalker was too strong a label to stick on T.C. He was sort of sweet. So was his friend, Scrubb.

Maybe calling him an extremely interested, awkwardly attentive acquaintance would be better. I don't know.

Still, why was I seconds away from engaging him in conversation?

I had no idea. Maybe because T .C. was willing to pay me? And I really needed the money.

Sure, or I'd gone completely nuts. That was always a strong possibility.

It's beyond creepy, which is ironic, given my bizarre gifting. Usually, I'm the one considered creepy. (More on that later.)

It truly takes one to know one. Maybe that's what drew him to me and me to him. We were both citizens on the fringe of normalcy. Perhaps it was our collective oddness that had me dialing his number.

Nah. It was definitely the money. My old van needed some love. Love disguised as a massive tune-up and new tires. That's why I risked it all and called T.C.

At least, that's what I kept telling myself. Too bad I'm not very convincing.

As the phone rang, I pulled Ace of Spades, my cat, to my side to comfort my pulsating nerves.

My tiny house, made from a converted VW Bus, usually made me feel safe and secluded. Instead, I felt naked and hunted.

It was all part of the price of speaking with T.C. I underestimated the effect giving into him would have on me. I debated hanging up the phone, there and then. But T.C. had already paid me well, and I had promised. I never broke a promise. Promises were all I had to hang on to.

"Penny, hello." T.C.'s overeager greeting made my feet itch.

I wanted to run. But there was nowhere to go. I was already home. I pulled Spades closer. The cat allowed me to squish him with only a meager hiss of disdain.

"Hello," I squeaked. Regret and panic nibbled on my waning confidence.

"I'm so glad you're willing to do this," T.C. said.

His voice didn't sound like it normally did when he was recording. On the Extra Extra Ordinary podcast, his excitable tenor smoothed out. It became velvety, authoritative, and self-assured.

Now, it reminded me of a Jr. High band nerd. The transition put me a bit more at ease. He wasn't any more certain about me than I was about him. That leveled the field.

"I'm not really sure what it is we're doing," I said. *Way to go, Captain Obvious*, I thought.

I stumbled over the right thing to say. I strove to project confidence and establish respect. Instead, I blurted out the first thing that came to me and opened myself up for ridicule and manipulation.

What else was new?

"Not to worry," T.C. said. "Scrubb is getting the recording equipment situated. It'll be a few minutes before we start. None of this is live. We splice and edit it and stick in a sponsor or two before it ever hits the listener's ears."

"Sponsors? Like commercials?" Flabbergasting. People paid to have their businesses advertised on T.C.'s conspiracy theory network.

T.C. chuckled on the other end of the call. "Crazy, isn't it? Yes, we currently have two sponsors. Both cater to our particular demographic."

Weirdoes, I thought but didn't say.

"Weirdoes," T.C. said. A morsel of pride simmered in his words. "I believe that's the common term for our followers."

Spades meowed loudly and scratched at me. He caught the soft spot of my wrist with one of his tiny cat talons. "Stop it!" I shooed him away. So much for being the comforting companion. Though mostly accommodating, sometimes my black cat friend had to remind me of his felineness.

"Sorry," I said to T.C. "My cat needs to roam." I shoved Spades out the passenger door of my van, AKA Godzilla, and rolled down the window.

Spades could finagle his way in through the tightest of spaces. He'd be back after a long prowl. Hopefully, before T.C. and I ended our chat. I could only guess that I'd need a good cuddle by then. Anxiety bubbled in my stomach and surged up my spine to knot on my shoulder blades. It was all I could do to keep breathing.

"We're nearly ready. How are you doing, Penny?" T.C. asked. He didn't realize the crushing weight of paranoia this one exchange was pushing on me. Pleased with himself and a bit cocky, he chatted with the podcast producer in the background.

"Okay, let's get cracking." I heard T.C. clap on the other side of the call. The casual tone he'd answered with melted away. A deliberately professional T.C. began our call. "You need a break? Let me know. Scrubb and I will piece our call together to make it as flattering as possible."

I cleared my throat. My mouth had suddenly become a desert. I chugged down a swallow of bottled water, only to choke and cough through the phone.

Things were about to get real. And I despised reality.

"How long do we have you?" T.C. asked.

Thanks to my stunning past self, I'd scheduled the call around working hours. If I was on and off the call as quickly as T.C. had promised, I could squeeze in a good cry and a nap before my shift.

Wishful thinking.

"30 minutes to an hour," I answered the madman on the other line.

"Great. Great," T.C. replied.

THE SESSION LASTED over ninety minutes. Spades returned and left again in that time. After circling restlessly around my ankles, he curled up on my driver's seat as I curled into the fetal position and rocked.

It hadn't been as bad as I'd dreaded. T.C. wanted to know the same things that I did.

Sadly, I couldn't give him answers I didn't have.

My so-called abilities were far beyond my understanding or control. Simply put, I saw things. Still do. Twinklings. Nudges. Glimpses of what the future might be. They were never good. Life just didn't work out that way. Not for me and not for the people I came in contact with.

These teeny peeks, into what would be, never came without caveats. Usually, doom followed on their heels. Doom and disaster. Of varying measure. After the mayhem, it was customary for me to either bear the blame or run terrified into the night.

T.C. was the first person to notice my strangeness and want to know more. Usually, even my best of friends charged off in the opposite direction. I didn't blame them. Not really. If I could, I would run away from these foreshadowings too.

I couldn't. I tried. They never left me alone for long.

In fact, I'd just escaped another encounter in a small town between Ashton and Lewiston called Pottersville. After witnessing two kidnappings, they snagged me too.

Thankfully, the town radiated with maternal instinct. A group of homeschool moms rescued and looked after me. I'd be crazy to think their kindness would last another round of the bad luck that follows me like a personal plague.

I'd made a friend in Pottersville. A strange old man, who had been my boss while I was there. I checked in with him once a month. Typically, by phone or email. Never face to face. The farther I stayed away from Mr. Joe, the better things would be for him.

This brought me back to being curled up in my tiny house on wheels, cradling my knees. I rolled there a few moments longer before dusting myself off, applying a smear of lip gloss, and heading to work.

Even a girl in exile needs to eat. As I'd discovered through the years, small businesses in small towns rarely checked references. There was usually some place that needed seasonal help, pronto. I was their gal.

The jobs were far from glamorous. They built up my experience, paid for my top ramen and cell phone, and kept Godzilla fed.

Rocky Grounds and Gifts was my newest place of employment. Mr. and Mrs. Rockland needed someone to roast, grind, and bag their seasonal coffee bean blends as they ran their shop.

Caffeine hung in the atmosphere. Just being near them and their quaint, homey store made every skin cell in my body buzz.

Opening the front door to start my shift blasted me with the smell of caramel, vanilla, and dark roast. If reading had a scent, I couldn't imagine a better match.

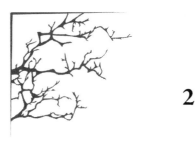

2

"THERE'S MY LUCKY PENNY," Mr. Rockland hollered from the back. My stomach churned. I hated whenever anyone called me that.

If they only knew.

"Terry burned the beans again," Mrs. Rockland whispered from behind the cash register.

Terry Rockland was not a pleasant person to encounter. Neither was his father. Not unless they needed something from you. Which they did.

From website maintenance to toilet bowl scrubbing, I was their go-to girl. As long as I ignored their awkward stares and murmured jabs at my weight, the status quo was tolerable.

Mrs. Rockland was the glittering gem of the trio. Genuinely a sweet person, she made working at Rocky Grounds bearable. Unfortunately, her husband and her son talked down to her and squelched her under their surveillance.

Mrs. Rockland locked the front door of the shop and flipped the Be Right Back sign over. "I don't know if we can save them. We'll have to start the order over."

I strapped on a Rocky Grounds apron and shoved my hair into a net.

Terry, the bean burner, sulked on his usual perch. Seated on a barstool at the edge of the kitchen's countertop, he could delegate and observe without getting his hands dirty. More than once, I'd felt his stare linger from his prominent place-creep-fest style.

I offered him what I hoped looked like a friendly smile that bubbled with boundaries. Judging by the Billy Idol sneer he returned, I'd failed. I stepped to Mrs. Rockland's side. Maybe an extreme interest in my work would prove my intense disinterest in Terry.

Mr. Rockland, Ken, if he was in a pleasant mood, stood festering beside the red coffee roaster. He stared into the drum as if staring into his own grave. I shuddered.

Grave was not the right word, or maybe it wasn't *his* grave he was looking into. Perhaps he'd reached the end of his patience with Terry and was about to carry out his ever-dangling threat of exile.

I doubted it.

Mrs. Rockland, Janice, as she wanted me to call her, rested a calm hand on Ken's forearm. "Why don't you scoot? Grab us something to eat. Penny and I will figure out this mess."

Ken shook off his anger. Janice to the rescue. His face softened. "Sure," he said.

"My purse is in my locker," Janice added. "Help yourself to some cash. Don't forget to pick up something for Penny, too."

I was about to object. I really didn't want to be obligated to anyone—especially cranky Ken and his sulky son.

Janice winked at me, silencing my argument.

Ken obeyed. Faster than I'd ever seen him move, he grabbed Janice's wallet and was out the door. Obviously, it was never his intention to help correct Terry's mishap. He'd been waiting for Janice to take over.

This was normal. Ken seemed to love basking in bankrolls and blaming others for the outgoing bills.

Work was better after Ken left. I wasn't complaining. He took me in without so much as an application. He paid me, decently, under the table and let me park Godzilla in their employee parking lot. Plus, I was only seasonal help. After the New Year, Rocky Grounds wouldn't need me anymore, and I'd move on.

It was a great deal for me. Moving on meant fewer people entangled in my mess. Six weeks of work, with no rent, could last me over a month. Maybe two, if I refrained from driving too much. I could keep Spades in kitty kibble and maintain my low-key social status. Perfect.

"You wanna tell me what happened?" Janice questioned Terry.

"He's a tyrant! That's what happened. That's what always happens." Terry crossed his arms and scowled.

Janice's shoulders tensed. "You know I don't let him talk about *you* that way. Please don't talk about *him* that way."

Terry glared at his mother. I shrunk back and scrubbed an already spotless counter.

"You didn't see him," Terry said.

Janice inspected the charcoaled beans, which were supposed to be roasted to a smooth medium. "How full was this when you started it?" She scooped the cremated beans from the drum and into a sterile canister. Then she fluttered over to the computer that programmed the roast and inspected its graphs.

"I know what I'm doing," Terry howled.

Sure he did, I thought. He knew just how to get out of the work.

Rocky Grounds had three huge custom orders to fill before the week's end. It meant hard work for all of us—beans, labels, packaging, shipping, and more. Manning the Grounds' storefront and brewing in the back would take everyone's help.

Terry responded to the impending hustle by overstuffing the small red drum and ruining the stock. All it took was a single ruined batch to slaughter profits, according to Ken.

Terry played his move well. Burning the first round meant Ken would send him away and leave the work to the rest of us.

Janice did just as Terry had hoped. He grinned and winked at me as he hugged his mom. "I'm so sorry," he apologized. "I tried my best, but I'm just not good enough for dad. Never have been."

Janice patted his head and coddled him for a moment. Even if Terry was closer to thirty than thirteen, his mother allowed his tantrum and sent him to restock shelves- a job I had already completed the night before.

Terry almost skipped from the kitchen. He cranked the store stereo and stayed out of Janice's eye line.

"Will you shut the door?" Janice nodded toward the employee-only entrance from the front to the back of Rocky Grounds. She didn't want to see Terry goof around any more than he wanted to be seen.

Janice rubbed her temples. Her dirty fingers left a sheen of coffee oil on her skin.

"Can you pull an all-nighter? With me?"

A smile cut through my resting beast face. "Of course," I said—anything to help Janice.

I received a grateful smile in return. "I'll pay you extra for your efforts," Janice added.

Inside, I squealed and clapped with excitement. After my stay with Rocky Grounds, I'd be able to score a new solar panel for Godzilla, as well as tires.

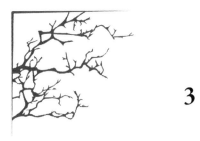

3

"YOU DO IT, THEN!"

The yelling from the front of the store overshadowed the slowly quieting rock music. Terry and Ken were not any more relaxed than when they'd parted ways.

The owner crashed through the employee's door, tossing curses back at his son. Ken took two hours to return with food, and he was not happy to be back.

"That boy of yours is killing our business." He tossed a bag of burritos on the kitchen island. It skidded across the stone-coated counter, nearly knocking over my neatly stacked piles of labels.

Janice's expression flickered between frustration and compassion. "Thanks, Hun," she said, referring to the sack that was already soggy with grease. She dusted her hands on her apron and planted a soft peck on Ken's cheek. "Burning a pound of beans will not close our doors."

Ken's cheeks puffed and reddened. "Keeping our doors closed will. The dolt didn't open. He was playing on his cell while customers waited outside."

"Really?" Janice said. "I'll go handle the customers." She hastily untied her apron.

"Don't bother. They took off when I unlocked the door, and that obscene music flooded out." Ken's face glistened with sweat.

"I'll go talk to him." Janice placed a hand on the door, but Ken halted her journey.

"He went home. Said he'd come back in the morning when we've calmed down," Ken told her.

Of course. By then, the work will be done. I thought as I continued cutting out labels. It was awkward being in the center of family fights.

"Who's gonna run the front?"

Ken shrugged his response to his wife.

"I'll go," Janice said. She turned back to me and pointed to the largest drum roaster. "That dark roast should finish in a minute. Let it cool. I'll get to it later."

I nodded. "You got it. I'll also finish the decaf orders. There are only three of them left."

Janice checked her vintage wristwatch. I glanced at the wall clock. One more hour until closing. Then the bulk of the work would begin.

"Come get me if you need anything," Janice said, first to Ken and then to me.

A stone plunked in the pit of my stomach. I was alone in the kitchen with Ken. He huffed and took up residence in his son's favorite seat.

The scent of spicy chicken, cool guacamole, and refried beans set my mouth watering. However, Ken's angry face warned me that slowing to eat was not what he had planned. I was a grunt, and he expected grunting, of the manual labor sort, from me.

I watched the coffee spin in its drum as it changed color. I had ninety seconds to fill the awkward silence. It ticked by like it was a hundred years.

If only there was something I hadn't already cleaned. The label printer alarmed. I jumped, which caused Ken to chuckle, proving he had been watching me from his perch. Goosebumps scattered like confetti along my skin.

The printer was nearer the office than the roasters. That meant I had to walk past Ken. Gratefully, I didn't feel his eyes follow me, and I didn't hear the chair squeak as he turned around. He must've been livid with Terry. The man wasn't himself. I wasn't sure if that was a good thing or a bad thing.

I retrieved the sheets of labels and returned to my workstation in time for the roaster to beep at me. Ken shot from his seat.

"Get it! Get it!" he hollered. It was sort of touching that he suddenly cared about the coffee. Terry's mishap might work to reveal a new side to the forward Mr. Rockland.

I hustled to put down the labels, far from the mess the beans would make. In a fluid rush, I shut off the roaster and spun open the hatch. A fresh nutty aroma steamed from the beans as they poured from the drum into the cooling bowl.

Ken clapped softly. "You are efficient for a chubby girl. I'll give you that."

The backward compliment hit me as Ken's attempt at humor. I offered only a nod in return. Apparently, that was the go signal for Ken Rockland.

"I'm glad we found you. Our Lucky Penny." I hated when he called me that. I hated when anyone called me that. Everyone did, at some point.

"Terry is a tool! That's what happens when a mother hen babies her chick. They never learn to fly for themselves," Ken spouted as he puffed around the kitchen.

No matter how hard I worked to be invisible, people loved to lay their life stories on me. Strangers, acquaintances, bosses. It didn't matter.

Here it was: the monologue. I prepared my ears and blank expression for the show. People dumped their drama onto my lap, no holds barred. It was weird. I was a stranger. A nobody. Though if I was honest, it made me feel a teeny bit useful. Even if I never paid close attention to the details.

Ken did not disappoint. "We sent him to school," he continued. "A local prep school and then a community college. He was supposed to learn all about business and help run this place. Instead, he scored solid Ds everywhere he went. Just enough to scrape by. But now we have you."

Oh, goodie, I thought.

He was, of course, referring to my low pay and high level of help. An investment in Penny Nicols was a great one.

As long as my "gifting" didn't rear its nasty head. It usually waited until I bonded with at least one person in town before it did that. For the moment, I was safe. So were my employers and their bankroll.

Since landing at Rocky Grounds, I'd revamped the website, restructured the novelty shelves, and set up an easy pay and ship program for the coffee.

That was on top of my everyday duties of dusting, sweeping, toilet plunging, and the rest of the nasty work. I didn't ask for insurance or vacation: just a job to do and the tools to do it well.

This made me a sound investment for the owners. My plus-sized body made me less of a threat to the owner's wives and girlfriends. Keeping work and home life separate and me as untangled as possible. Everyone stayed happy as long as I got out of town before my secret settled in.

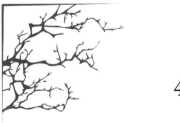

4

KEN'S STORY WASN'T far from unusual. Though he surprised me when he said, flat out, that he didn't love Janice. I couldn't see how he couldn't love Janice. She took care of him and caved to him endlessly. Maybe that was it. Maybe he didn't like the mothering tenderness she displayed.

I could only imagine what motherly tenderness would feel like.

My mother had died when I was still small. In fact, all I remember of her comes from stories and a single photograph of her with my father. His hands were on her pregnant belly, and she was laughing. The shimmer of happy tears sparkled in the corner of her eyes.

Though I couldn't remember her, I missed her more than made sense. It was probably best she didn't live to see who or what I'd become.

In Ken's case, he had someone right in front of him offering him love, and he sneered at it. His bitter words hurt me for Janice.

"Then Terry came along and poof... being married wasn't fun anymore. When you toss a howling kid into it and a wife who has lost her looks, when she had them, it's barely tolerable."

Ken's piercing honesty and hard eyes had my guts shaking. I had to avoid meeting his gaze while I worked in hopes he'd trail off and leave me alone.

I poured the fresh hot beans into metal cooling bowls, labeled paper bags, and sorted decorative aluminum clips.

"My advice," he said as I ladled Terry's burned batch into the grinder and set it to espresso. "Don't do it. The whole marriage thing. It's a crock."

Before Ken could say anything, I switched on the industrial grinder. I didn't want to know. I didn't want to hear.

Time, though sluggish at spots, went by faster than I could have wished. It overjoyed me when Janice popped back into the kitchen and announced she'd locked up for the day.

"Penny, why didn't you eat your burrito?" she asked as she opened the fridge and pulled out the lunch sack.

"I couldn't get her to take a break," Ken lied. How he did it so easily was unnatural. "I begged her to slow down. But she's a workhorse. It was hard keeping up with her."

From the tired smile reflecting in Janice's eyes, it was easy to see she wasn't buying Ken's bologna.

"Penny, why don't you nuke both?" Janice asked. "I'm starved."

I happily took the sack. Janice turned to face Ken. "And you, handsome, why don't you head home? Maybe split a pizza with Terry and watch one of those bust 'em up movies together? Penny and I have a long job ahead of us."

"I don't know. You two ladies shouldn't be here, alone, at night." Ken's voice was sincere, but he nearly bounced at the prospect of bolting.

"You'll stay and help?" Janice asked, a little more eagerly than her face displayed.

Ken's eyes darted. "You know I want to, but..."

"Shh. You don't have to say it. I can see it on your face. You're worried about Terry. What a sweetheart!" She stood on her toes and kissed him.

Ken didn't seem that unhappy of a husband as he returned the kiss. He didn't pause, afterward, to say goodbye. As soon as Janice's kiss ended, so did Ken's work shift.

Janice returned to the kitchen, locking up after Ken, as I pulled out our burritos. She clapped her hands and dished out two paper plates and two bottles of pop.

We ate in near silence. Both of us were exhausted. Me: from my conversation with T.C. and my avoidance of Ken. She, I guessed, from running a store single-handedly but pretending she wasn't.

The burritos were filling and scrumptious, despite the soggy tortillas and microwaved shredded lettuce. They were wonderful compared to my main fare of a cup of noodles and an apple for dessert.

I wondered how Spades was handling the fall of night, then laughed to myself. Nighttime was his time. He was probably prowling around and wooing unsuspecting house cats. Chomping on whatever delicacies he could scavenge. Spades was a loner, like me. It was one reason we got on so well.

Janice finished her food and cleared our disposables. I downed the last swallow of soda and squared my shoulders.

"We've got fifteen pounds to go for tonight. All dark," Janice announced after counting up the work I'd already completed. She yawned. I struggled not to mirror her sleepiness. "Let's get to work so we can get to bed."

"You got it," I said, as I mentally buckled down for a difficult few hours.

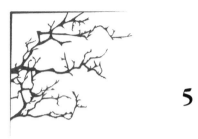

5

"DO WE NEED MORE LABELS?" I asked over the grinder grating.

Janice shook her head. Working together, we rhythmically roasted and cooled beans. We scooped them into three-ounce cardboard tubes and labeled them with silver and yellow wedding party labels.

Janice bundled the bunches into groups of eight to match table settings. "This will make it so much easier for the wedding planner to separate," she explained as she placed each bundle into a paper bag bearing the Rocky Grounds logo.

How she could put others first while being bullied by her own family was beyond me. But Janice did. Usually with a smile on her face. I wanted to blurt out, "How do you do it?" but didn't dare. It wasn't any of my business and would only wrap me further up into the lives of my employers. Lives that I'd be leaving soon- hopefully unscathed. I brushed my hair in front of my face, ever so slightly, to hide my thoughtful expression.

Too late.

"They're not so bad," Janice said. "They're just of that age."

"What age?" I hadn't meant to speak out loud, so I hadn't toned down the snarky edge to my voice.

Twenty-five-ish and forty-five-ish were two gigantic leaps away from similar stages in maturity. It was more like two grown men who loved dodging responsibility and were constantly throwing shade on anything resembling adulting.

I wasn't twenty yet and had clawed out a life for myself. Not a big one or even moderately sized either. But it was mine, and I took responsibility for it. Even when that meant having a wild cat as my only companion, two strange cyber pen-pals, and an old man, towns away, who told me he prayed for me. Still, I had made a life.

Ken and Terry sucked the life out of others.

Janice's long lingering sigh said as much. She rubbed her neck and dusted chaff from her apron. It wafted upwards and landed on the top of her glasses frame.

"I haven't figured it out. As far as I can tell, men grow up in clusters. They'll plod along for about three years in a state of nonchalance, and then the next five will be all brooding and disaster. I think they've both hit their angsty stages at the same time." Janice stuck out her bottom lip and puffed the rogue silver skin from her face.

"I still don't understand it," I said.

"Honey, we're women. We're not meant to. We just live with it until it feels like we're going to break, and then we bloom."

"What does that mean?"

Janice made a loose fist and shook it in front of her nose. "It means we get stronger. And we grab hold of every advantage nature has given us."

I felt my eyebrow raise to match Janice's. Stronger? I liked the sound of that. But not if that meant handling more masculine annoyances.

A soft knock interrupted our chat. "That'll be Jack." Janice scooted from the room with a bounce in her step.

Jack, the Grounds' delivery man, was half a decade younger than Janice if he was a day. That didn't stop the two of them from flirting. Neither did the fact that both of them were married.

Still, I couldn't hold it against Janice. With Grumpy and Grumpier living and working alongside her day in and out, a friend was exactly what she needed. Even if the friendship teetered on the edge of something more.

I'd met Jack twice. He was handsome, pleasant, and kind. A lot like Janice, from what I could tell. His hinting side glances never progressed to awkwardness. The relationship remained platonic, in a physical sense, if not an emotional one.

I'd seen affairs like this before. They did damage. Just like their physical counterparts. Except sneakier. They gave their participants false security and a fake high horse to ride on. They promised hope for more while maintaining one's self-righteousness.

I hated seeing Janice dipping her toe in the dangerous waters that intense feelings churned up. What could I say? She was an adult, after all.

Janice left the door between the store and the kitchen open. She always did this when Jack dropped by.

Perhaps for a sense of decency, I thought, when I heard her unlock the front door and let him in.

"It's cold out there," she said as the wind followed her visitor inside the store.

It must've been rather blustery. A chill swept through the front, through the smoky kitchen, and up my hoodie sleeves. I shuddered.

"It looks like it might rain again," Jack remarked. I imagined his happy blue eyes looking deeply into Janice's dark gray ones. His hands respectively contained in his pockets. His usual stance.

"It's normal for this time of year," Janice said dumbly.

I peeked at the security monitor, curiosity getting the better of me. Janice was gesturing with a side glance at the kitchen door. She was gently alerting Jack that a witness was nearby. They'd keep their conversation to the weather as long as I was in earshot.

"If you're done, soon, I can follow you home," Jack offered.

Janice hesitated to respond. She flashed a look toward the security camera and right at me. My stomach churned.

Our work was technically finished. Janice had packaged the last of the party favors. We completed basic cleanup. The nightly floor scrubbing that Mr. Rockland demanded was the only box left to check off.

"Let me get my purse," Janice said.

She returned to the kitchen with a warm glow on her cheeks. "Penny," she started, blushing. "Would you mind if we met early in the morning to finish cleaning? Mr. Rockland and Terry aren't due for their shifts until the afternoon. You and I could get this work done before then."

I didn't want to come to work early. I also didn't enjoy being a party to whatever Jack's walk home entailed. If Ken or Terry found out and took their bullying from verbal to physical, I wouldn't know what to do.

However, I also didn't want to disappoint Janice. She'd been so kind to me and understanding. I owed her kindness in return.

"Sure," I responded.

I quickly washed my hands and grabbed my backpack.

Jack's workman boots clomped in the shop. He was pacing in gray scale on the security screen.

I motioned to the monitor, but before I could question Janice, she said, "I'll delete the security feed tomorrow morning before Terry comes in. He never notices when time is missing."

I nodded. "Front door? Back door?" I wasn't sure which exit Janice preferred me to take.

She led me to the back door and opened it. I squeezed between her arm and the door frame.

"Thanks, Penny," she whispered as if I'd just smuggled her a forbidden pastry. Then, with a happy weariness in her eyes, she locked me out of Rocky Grounds Coffee and Gifts.

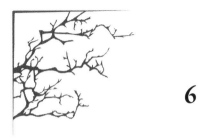

6

"PUMPKIN SPICE LATTE!" I cursed. The cold air bit through my jacket.

The wet whipping wind inspired me to sprint to Godzilla. I slid open the van door, entered, and slammed it closed behind me. It wasn't much warmer inside. However, it was dry.

It was too late in the season to leave a window cracked for Spades all night. He scowled at me from the driver's seat, where he'd burrowed beneath my favorite blanket.

I shrugged off my jacket but didn't bother putting on pajamas. I was too cold. If it weren't so late, I would've driven to the gym for a nice hot shower before bed. Alas, small-town gyms closed early in the winter. A decent scrub down would have to wait for tomorrow afternoon.

I pulled my curtains closed and curled up on the couch. At the clicking of the dial on my heated blanket, Spades hustled over and took his place at my feet. In a few minutes, we'd both be warm enough to drift off to sleep.

I texted myself a reminder to ask Janice if I could plug into the shop's outside power. During the day, my solar panels kept things running. At night, in winter, there just wasn't enough stored light to keep the heater chugging.

If I could plug in, I could run my tiny electric heater and not worry about draining my battery. For now, my electric blanket with automatic shut-off would have to do. It would ward off the worst of the frigidity, and body heat would do the rest.

Just like every other night, I both longed for and dreaded sleep. There was no telling and no controlling what might happen in my dreams. The saddest and scariest of my thoughts often attacked my resting mind in crazed clusters. Especially when I was the most exhausted. I took a deep cleansing breath and focused on the sound of Spades purring until the worries of the day faded away into blackness.

A LOUD RAPPING ON THE van's back door sent Spades hissing and clawing around the van. I grabbed him before he could damage himself and received another deep scratch across my wrist in return.

"Thanks a bunch," I scolded my twitchy houseguest as I applied pressure to the stinging red welts swelling on the softest part of my arm.

There wasn't a rush of sunlight when I parted the back curtains. Only Janice's smiling face. If it was morning already, it was much too early for real life to begin.

"One minute," I called.

"Get dressed," Janice commanded through the glass. "The diner just opened, and I'm buying you breakfast."

My stomach rumbled in response—first a free dinner and now breakfast. I could get used to eating consistent meals. Ones whose selling point wasn't "just add water."

I flashed her an up thumb and closed the curtain.

"Okay, Spades," I said to my reckless cat. "I'll be back to let you out. Be good," I coached my fellow vagabond as I changed clothes, slathered on deodorant, and quickly tamed my red hair.

Then, just in case, I set a small kitty litter tray on the passenger seat. Spades glowered at me.

I was out of the van in less than five minutes.

Janice was pacing and clapping her hands against her arms. Fog puffed with her every breath. "That was fast," she commented, and linked my arm with hers.

I locked the doors and tucked the keys into my hoodie pocket. It was too cold to sport my jersey jacket solo. I wore my hoodie beneath my winter coat.

"You learn how to get dressed quickly when it's cold," I said.

Janice laughed. She led me down the road toward the Overeasy Diner. Its neon sign flickered in hot pink and orange. Though the windows hosted frost around the edges, I could spot diners already at booths.

"What time is it?" I asked.

"A little after six," Janice said as she held open the front door.

She led me to a corner booth, at least two tables away from the closest diners. There was a bounce in her step. Impending good news bubbled and boiled within her, just waiting to spill over and out.

I sat, suddenly filled with trepidation. My eyes were blurring from sleep. The sudden waking didn't do me any good either. I needed coffee, pronto. The very thought of it made me sleepier.

Janice snickered at me. "Rough night?" she asked, not expecting me to answer, as she was already flagging down a waitress. "Hey, Betty Fae," she called. "Coffee before we order, please."

"You've got it, Toots," the waitress hurried over with two mugs and a carafe.

The heat from the coffee was delicious. I felt myself becoming more human with each tiny sniff and sip.

"Better?" Janice asked, watching me closely.

"Much," I answered, my palms spooning the chunky mug.

"I thought I'd treat you to waffles and chicken for breakfast. Does that sound good?"

"More than good."

"Great," Janice said. She placed the order across the room just as she'd asked for the coffee. "Afterwards, we'll go scrub the kitchen and box the order. Jack is coming by to pick it up at 7:30."

I tried to restrain my busy body smirk when Janice mentioned Jack. But we were face to face. I couldn't dodge Janice's attention.

"Don't worry about me," my boss said. "I know what I'm doing."

"Do you?"

Janice sipped her coffee and dropped her voice to whisper, "I know what the gossip is, but Jack and I are just great friends."

I adjusted my flatware, ignoring the blatant lie.

"Seriously," Janice said. "That's all. He'd like us to be more. At least I think he would, but he's married. I'm married. It will not happen."

Betty Fae set steamy plates of chicken and waffles on the table before setting down a can of whipped cream and two jugs of heated syrup. "Maple and blueberry," she stated, and turned back to the rest of the cafe.

"Mmm, blueberry syrup is my favorite." Janice drowned her waffle in the dark purple liquid.

I opted for butter- carefully cutting and filling each waffle square with a dollop before sprinkling it lightly with maple syrup.

I watched Janice dip a chicken thigh in the blue syrup before eating it. She did a happy jig. "Yum. Yum," she commented. "The boys never want to wake up early enough to get breakfast. And I hate eating alone. I'm glad you came with me."

"Thanks for treating me," I said, sliding a knife through the crunchy waffle crust.

"It's my pleasure." Janice grabbed the red can of cream and held it upside down above her coffee cup. "Truly, though," she continued. "Jack and I are nothing to be embarrassed or concerned about. At least not anymore."

Anymore? I thought. *What had happened during her walk home?* I kept my wonderings to myself, hoping she'd fill in the blanks, so my imagination didn't have to.

Janice didn't fail me. She started explaining immediately. "I told him," she said, as she squirted whipped cream on the top of her mug. Making a spiral mountain, she replaced the can with a spoon and stirred her drink. The cream deflated and drifted around her coffee. "Even if we have feelings for each other, that's no excuse for pretending we can do anything about them."

"And he's okay with it?" I asked, before chewing on the most delicious waffle I'd had in my life. My taste buds rollicked in pleasure with each bite.

"Not okay, exactly," Janice said. "It won't kill him."

Her words scratched at my conscience like sand stuck in a damp swimsuit. They felt wrong and dangerous.

Janice continued, "The last few weeks... Shortly after you arrived, tensions spiked. I don't understand why. Things have pressurized intensely in every area of my life. Terry's derailing, rapidly. Jack's asking for more of my attention. Then there's Ken. His acting is off. He runs off every Wednesday and pretends like it's no big thing. Says he's fishing. Jokes that it's his version of therapy. I'm not buying it. He's wading knee-deep in troubled waters."

I frowned at my breakfast. If what I'd witnessed was Ken's act, what was his genuine self like? I shivered to think of it.

It wasn't my place to reveal my own judgments about Terry, Jack, or Ken. Janice hadn't asked. I desperately hoped she wouldn't. I wasn't good at honesty if I also needed to tenderfoot around other people's feelings. Tact has never been my specialty. That's one reason I often opt for invisibility.

My primary concern was Janice's timeline. The last few weeks? Shortly after I arrived? Was the cycle starting? Already?

Shrugging off the foreboding that was building within me, I dove back into my breakfast. It was the holiday season, after all. Life was a rollercoaster this time of year. Maybe it had nothing to do with me? A girl could pretend, couldn't she?

Janice said something about threats against the shop that caught my attention. I risked a glance at her worried yet cheerful face.

"I've talked to the other shop owners. They've received the same calls. The police know about them. I guess that's all I can do about that. I can't risk Terry and Ken even suspecting Jack and me. Not that there is a Jack and I." Her last statement faded to a hush.

I'd missed something. "What do prank calls have to do with Ken and Terry?"

Janice took a drink of her creamy coffee. "Oh, nothing. I'm just more paranoid than I need to be. If someone vandalizes the shop, the police could take my security feed. They could notice the timestamp discrepancies. I don't want to cast a shadow on Jack's reputation by saying he was there, and that's why I changed the video. The police are bound to ask."

She was right, they would ask. "Jack's your delivery guy. If everything between you guys is as innocent as you say, what does it matter if he's at the shop?"

Janice took another sip before placing her cup on the table. "Things are innocent, and they'll stay that way. Jack's always been a good friend. Until his wife disappeared a few months ago, our bond was one of consolation and mutual understanding. That doesn't mean that's how everyone else will see it. Small towns can have big gossips."

Boy, did I know that! More than my share of small towns chased me out of their limits. I still didn't think Janice had as much to worry about as she thought. She was the apple of Main Street's eye. The tenderhearted shopkeeper with the terrible family situation. It might get rocky if her flirtation with Jack hit the streets, but she'd skate through it. The town's dislike of Ken would see to that.

I was about to say so, to encourage her, when Janice dabbed at a small spill from her coffee cup. Having captured my distracted mind, her coffee was now all I could think about.

There, winking at me from Janice's beige coffee cup, was the very thing I dreaded most. Forming from the leftover foam of her whipped topping, a perfectly shaped raven floated on her beverage.

I choked on my waffle.

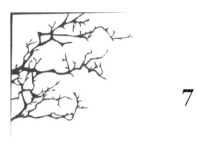

7

IT WASN'T LIFE THAT flashed before my eyes as Betty Fae thwacked me between the shoulder blades. It was death and disaster—replays of all the faces of shock and sadness worn by acquaintances of my past. Death of one sort or the other followed that stupid Raven.

I remembered them all. Vividly. The writer, the homeschool mom, the surfer, the politician. They were among the near-strangers I'd encountered and endangered.

Following their faces came the really painful pictures. The friendly child advocate, the sweet boy next door, and losing my aunt and uncle. After them, but always above them, followed the loss of my sister and father.

All because of the same intolerable bird. Gracious enough to give me a glimpse of their perils before nudging them to the brink. Impending doom sat, staring at me, from the cup of the only friend I had in town- Janice Rockland. It lingered there amid the froth bubbles, telling me Janice Rockland had twenty-four hours, at most, left to live.

My eyes watered. My throat closed all the tighter. Even after it dislodged my Belgian waffle. Air battled past my suffocating emotions. I gulped it down, despising myself and fearing for my boss.

Janice and Betty Fae offered me a glass of water and napkins, thinking they'd saved the day. Little did they know. Trouble had just landed in their small town.

Janice watched me through the rest of the meal. If I told her she was about to die, would she be able to eat? I sipped my coffee and avoided conversation.

Long ago, I'd explained my weird glimpses to one of the Raven's victims. Instead of believing me, my friend grew increasingly sarcastic about my confession. He mocked me. I didn't blame him. I'm not sure I would've believed me, either. In the end, his sarcasm killed him.

Laughing and gesturing like a mad bird to make fun of my premonitions, he'd lost control of his bicycle and collided with a garbage truck just as it was lowering its load.

No, I wasn't about to tell Janice about her Raven. I'd keep watch. Stay sharp. Once the bird made an appearance, he wouldn't leave until his prey was dead. Accidentally or with malice aforethought.

The next song, movie quote, television commercial, or anything ominous could clue me in on how to save her. At least I could give it a shot. If I didn't keep a constant eye on Janice, her death would be on my head.

"Add it to your list."

It startled me. The Raven hadn't spoken to me before. I was really losing it.

Janice leaned across the table and tapped my wrist. "Earth to Penny," she said.

"Huh?"

She smiled. "Still dazed from your near-death experience? I would be." She wiped her face and placed her napkin on her dish. "I was just asking if, along with cleaning and packing, could you add reordering to your list?"

Relief flooded over me. Was it strange that I was happy I was only slightly crazy and not hearing voices?

"Sure," I answered.

Janice flagged down Betty Fae and handled the check. I slipped the only cash I had on me under my coffee cup as a tip for dealing with my momentary freakout.

As Janice bundled up, Betty Fae hit the jukebox remote. I held my breath as it hummed to life.

"Please play something nice," I whispered to myself.

No dice. *Last Kiss* started playing.

"Great song! But not breakfast music," Janice said, tossing a tip in the jar next to the register.

Betty Fae frowned and pushed another button. The jukebox shuffled. *Leader of the Pack* blasted right at its climax.

My stomach dropped. Unless I could keep her away from all traffic and roads, Janice was doomed.

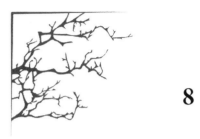

8

OUTSIDE, THE MORNING chill had turned into a frost. The sidewalk was slick beneath my sneakers. Janice wrapped herself in a hug and shivered. "My, my, my," she said. "Let's get to the shop and get the kitchen warmed up. It's only going to get colder."

Mania flicking at my mind made me laugh aloud. It was only going to get colder for Janice if I didn't straighten up. I focused on getting Janice out of the street and inside a building. By the thematic choice of jukebox hits, all highways, byways, roadways, and freeways were off-limits if I wanted to keep her alive.

"Do you need to let Spades out?" Janice asked me.

I flinched. "Yes, but I'll hurry."

"Take your time," Janice said. "I'll go inside and get things going. Come in through the back," she added as she reached for the door handle. "I'll unlock the door for you."

"Great. Thanks," I said, letting a premature smile rest on my face.

I sprinted to Godzilla, skidding as I went. Spades snarled at me when I ripped open the door and let the wet air in. I scooped him up and tossed him to the asphalt.

"Do your business," I ordered.

My sudden brashness startled Spades. He shook it off and sauntered away slowly. I was on to him. He didn't want me to believe my opinion mattered to him. I knew better.

We were a band of outcasts and bosom friends. He'd be pouty later, to punish me. For now, I hoped he'd hustle his skinny tail back to the van.

Inside, I quickly did my daily chores. With the wind moving, I couldn't place the solar panel out like normal. I did the next best thing and propped it up against the windshield to soak in what sun squeezed through the glass. It wouldn't be much.

Hurriedly, I connected what needed to be charged, shoved my tablet and phone into my backpack, and wedged a bottle of calming essential oil under my bra strap. It was going to be a rough 24 hours. Hyperventilating would not help. The oil could relax my nerves before they got the better of me if I remembered to use it.

Spades shot past me. Flecks of weather shook from his body as he charged past my head and straight for my pillow.

"Gross," I said. Wet cat scent and rain puddles were soaking into my favorite pillow and laundry day wasn't even close. "I hope you got it all out. Because I'm locking you in." Spades spat at me. I stuck my tongue out at him in return.

I hopped from the van and hustled inside the back door of the shop. Janice was sitting in front of the security laptop, erasing Jack from last night, no doubt. I hung up my coat and jacket and washed my hands. It was still far too early for the shop to open.

Janice didn't greet me or start barking orders. There was no need. I already knew what my tasks were for the day. It was time to scrub. The clumsy orange mop bucket kicked me in the Achilles tendon as I dragged it to the mop sink. Pouring a capful of cleaner into the running water, I waited.

That's when I noticed Janice sitting stalk still. Frozen. I hadn't realized she was acting odd when I'd come inside. She wasn't moving. Not a muscle. She wasn't typing or scrolling or jotting down notes for the day.

She sat riveted to the screen.

I walked over to her, but an odd feeling overtook me—the presence of fear. A lingering sense of exposure crept along my shoulders.

From my side-eye, I saw the office door was ajar, as usual. Except papers littered every inch of the tiny space. My head spun as my breath caught back up with me. I pulled out my calming oil and sniffed it without unscrewing the cap. Something was very wrong.

"Janice," I whispered. "What's going on?"

Her voice was steady even as her expression verged on wild hysteria. "We've been hit. By the vandals." She pointed toward the front.

I walked into a room of mess. Dumped shelves, tossed greeting cards peppered the floor, far from where I'd left them the night before.

"Aren't you going to call the police?" I asked her, afraid to touch anything.

Janice followed me slowly. "What good would it do?" She bent and retrieved a Rocky Grounds coffee mug.

"You really shouldn't be touching that," I stated.

"I told you, I'm not calling the police. Besides," Janice said, spinning around slowly, "nothing's broken. Even the register is fine. The cash drawer is in the safe. There's been no actual damage."

I stammered, "I'm not sure you should..."

"Penny, it's fine. I know what I'm doing. Let's just get this mess cleaned up before Ken comes. He'll lose it if he sees this."

I obeyed. It wasn't my place to argue.

Thankfully, the store was on the smaller side. Their biggest seller was their roasted coffee beans. The vandals hadn't touched that section.

It was strange as I unrighted and refilled shelves, turning labels toward the shoppers' eye line. They hurt nothing. Not a single mug or candle. Even the cards were remarkably undamaged.

The longest job was sorting which envelope went with which greeting card. None of them were bent or torn. Not one bore a shoe print or a rainwater smudge. I'd witnessed vandalism before. This attack was wild. It made no sense. These were the tidiest band of rogues I'd ever seen.

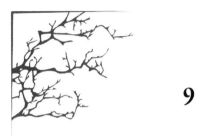

9

A SOFT HONK FROM A passing car interrupted me. I spun in circles, tracking my boss's whereabouts.

"It's just Jack." She sniffled. "He said he'd honk before pick up. Will you help me?"

Jack wasn't the only one having a hard time with the pre-relationship breakup. Janice missed him, too.

I piled two boxes on top of each other and followed Janice to the front door.

"We're going to leave them on the curb," she said. "Then he doesn't have to come in. The honk was to tell me we're next on his route."

"But it's just about to rain," I said, desperate to keep Janice away from the street.

"It'll be alright," she said. "We'll place them under the awning."

I trudged loads behind Janice as quickly as I could- always staying a step behind her. I didn't want to leave her alone for a single second.

When our last load sat expectantly on the sidewalk, I clapped.

"Yeah," Janice said as she glanced oddly at me. "Finishing an enormous job feels great, doesn't it?'

"I guess," I replied.

Janice resumed her position at the monitor. Safe and sound. I took up my place at the mop station. Water splashed down the side of the pail as I plunged the mop head beneath the soapy hot water. It splattered on the floor, leaving the outline of a black-winged bird in its wake.

My breath seized. Quickly, I shoved it away as if it were only grime and scrubbing it would make it, and everything it stood for seep down the drain.

The security monitor barstool squeaked. I glanced up. Janice snagged a small cardboard box from the countertop beside her.

"I forgot," she said as she ran out to the curb. I dropped the mop. Its handle clattered on the ground behind me. I chased after her.

Janice placed the small box atop the others. I was a room away.

The box teetered and bounced onto the road. I was at the door.

Janice stepped off the sidewalk. I jerked the door open.

Headlights sliced through the morning darkness and landed on Janice. She froze, almost smiling at the lights. I screamed and launched myself at her.

The horn of a passing vehicle blared and faded as it crushed the small parcel and continued down the road, inches from the heels of my sneakers. I stretched to retrieve my phone and snapped a photo of the retreating license plate.

Janice's heartbeat thudded near my ear. I caught my breath and slid off my boss and smack into a puddle of sludge.

I scanned Janice from my soggy seat. There wasn't any blood. No bones stuck through the skin. No bruises swelled. Next to her, shimmering in the glow of Rocky Grounds main interior light, a puddle raven dissolved and drifted into the air. Had I done it? Had I really saved Janice?

"Are you okay?" I asked her when my breath returned.

Janice's gray eyes blinked, slow and steady. Her expression was unreadable. Shock? Fear? Pain? Relief? Every emotion I could name flickered and shifted in only a moment.

"What have you..." she started. "What did you... How am I..."

Janice propped herself up on her elbows and examined me. "You're bleeding," she stated. "And soaked. Let's get you out of the street."

An old clunky blue truck skidded up to Rocky Grounds. Just as hastily, the driver shut it off and hurried out of the car.

I braced myself. Janice was still in the middle of the road. She was still in danger.

Jack kneeled beside her on the hard ground. His hands trembled as his lips went pale. His eyes mimicked Janice's random slideshow of emotions.

"What happened?" he questioned her.

I rose shakily. Embedded in the meat of my palms were tiny pebbles. I plucked them out and tossed them back to the ground.

Jack took Janice under her elbows and lifted her to her feet. She was much steadier than I was. With Jack acting as ballast, why wouldn't she be?

The three of us limped out of the road and under the awning. Jack retrieved the destroyed box and handed it to me. I cradled it, more to calm myself than to protect it.

"Do you need help? Should I call the paramedics? The police? Ken?" Jack choked up on the last word.

"I've already called Ken." Betty Fae, from the diner, was suddenly next to us. She must've seen everything from her front register.

Janice's shoulders pinched closer to her ears. It took a long exaggerated exhale to get them to relax.

"Thank you, Jack," Janice said. A cool edge fractured her gratitude. She *was* serious about giving up on Jack. "We're fine. We're going to get cleaned up before opening. There are the day's deliveries." Janice extended an index finger toward the pile of bundles.

His eyes stammered with sadness. Janice dismissed him. Possibly forever. Instead of arguing and prolonging the situation, he simply placed two fingers to the brim of his cap and saluted a farewell. Then Jack hoisted the boxes into his delivery truck and drove away.

Janice didn't even watch him go.

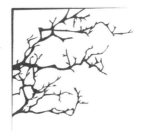

10

KEN BLAZED THROUGH the front door, charged through the gift shop, and straight into the kitchen. He stared at me as my clothes dripped a muddy puddle all over the tile. Words of disgust trailed behind his eyes.

I didn't blame him, but there was little I could do. We were still waiting for the police to show up. I couldn't go clean up before giving my statement. That would mean leaving the scene. I'd been there before, and it wasn't pretty.

I stood alone and worried, with my clothes stiffening into a crusty shield around me. I itched to get clean. Itched to get to my van and drive away before the bird made more trouble for Janice.

Ken stopped glaring at me and turned, looking for his wife. She was sitting in his favorite chair. Not as dirty as I was, but quite a deal more banged up.

The blood Janice saw wasn't mine. It added up to not much more than a scratch on her left hand, but it was enough to require pressure. Janice held a clean kitchen towel over her hand and stared into the blank space before her.

Ken's face fell at the sight of his wife's shock. He stumbled nearer and awkwardly wrapped his arms around her. Janice let him, though she didn't return the embrace. She rested her head gingerly on Ken's bicep.

"I'm okay," she said. "I'm okay."

Betty Fae rolled her eyes. "Police should be here soon." She turned, looking at me for the first time since her arrival. "Appears Penny, saved her."

Ken's shoulders shook. Was he crying? He was an excellent actor.

The front door's welcome bell clanged as the first officer entered the shop.

"We're back here, Fred," Betty Fae called.

Fred sauntered into the kitchen. His cowboy boots echoed on the floor. He gave me the same look over Ken had and then turned to the Rocklands. "Who wants to talk first?"

Betty Fae monologue'd as a paramedic joined the crowd. The newcomer immediately tended to Janice. He checked her eyes, head, and neck before moving on to her palm.

"This is going to need stitches," he stated flatly. "We can drive you to the local hospital if you'd like?"

Ken touched his wife on the shoulder with more tenderness than I imagined he possessed. It confused me. And Janice. She shivered under the attention.

"I'll take her," Ken said. "As soon as we finish with the police. We need to find out exactly who tried to do this to Janice."

Suddenly, Janice found her voice. "Do this to me? Nobody did this to me! It was an accident."

"Only because Penny shoved you out of the way." Ken's volume rose as his emotions did. "If she hadn't been there." He turned his back on the group, hiding his sorrow behind the kitchen door.

Was Ken Rockland actually crying? What was going on?

"Are you Penny?" Fred, the policeman, turned to me as if just noticing there was a person behind the mud.

"That's her," Betty Fae said. "Seems like today is the day for second chances and near-death experiences." The waitress cackled.

My knees caved, and I felt myself slowly fade to the ground, crashing into the mop bucket along the way.

THEY FORCED ME TO GO to the ER, but once I was there, I refused any treatment. I was fine! Really! At least that's what I told everyone who pawed at me. I just wanted to go home.

There was no way the Raven was leaving me alone. Last time, the only time I'd bypassed his fatal feathers, someone else had paid the price. Saving Janice might have set in motion an elaborate domino course. One that ended in fire, smoke, and other man-made disasters.

I needed to rest. Get changed. Get my mind right- even though every morsel of self-preservation within me wanted to flee. I couldn't. Not until everyone was safe.

Janice was wrong. The incident in the street hadn't been an accident. Someone had set their aim and smashed down the accelerator. That person, like a pesky bird of prey, wouldn't stop with a narrow escape.

Ken caught sight of me as he paced outside the hospital. He rushed over to me. "Did you see her?"

I shook my head. Why was he asking *me*? He should be with Janice.

"She wouldn't let me stay beside her. Janice knows I hate the sight of blood and the thought of hospitals. She sent me out here to wait. But I'm going crazy." Ken waved his hands wildly in the air to solidify his point.

"She'll be okay," I lied.

"Thank you, Penny. Thank you."

Then Ken did something off-putting and frightening. He hugged me. In huge papa bear style, he squeezed me until I couldn't breathe.

Was this the same man who wasn't in love with his wife? The one who called marriage a crock? When I didn't respond, Ken took the cue and backed away. Tears streamed down his haggard face.

"I've called Terry," he said. "I didn't tell him when Betty Fae called earlier. Before I woke him, I wanted to see what was happening. He's on the way. He'll take you to our house and let you get cleaned up."

Shock washed over me. Kindness made me nervous. Kindness from previously peevish people made me outright paranoid. "I'm fine," I said. "I'll go home and-"

"No. No. Terry will take you home to grab your clothes. Then he'll drop you at my house so you can shower and change." Ken was being friendly, but I couldn't bring myself to be grateful. Strings were dangling somewhere. I could sense them. "Then he'll come back here and see his mom. We only live a few blocks from the shop. You could walk there and open it for us."

There it was. Thunk. The other shoe dropped. Someone needed to run Rocky Grounds, and I was the only employee that wasn't family. No break for Penny. It was better that way. Too much downtime was never a good idea. Not for me.

"Sure," I said. "Why not?"

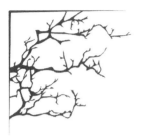

11

TERRY CHARGED FULL pedal over every speed bump in the residential area. He grunted at me. Randomly spouting disgust in my direction.

"Things were fine. Fine," he gibbered. I scooted as close to my door as I could without falling out of the moving vehicle. "I had a plan. And now. You ruined it!"

I cradled my backpack. Being alone with Terry was less than comforting.

"Dad says you saved Mom. So I guess you'd expect me to be grateful."

Yes, I thought. *Yes, I would.*

Though it remained to be seen if I'd truly saved anyone, the storm brewing above the town kept live birds from exposing themselves. That didn't mean my foul weather friend would stay hidden.

"I'm not grateful. She would have been better off as roadkill. Living with dad, like this, is the worst."

My mouth ran off without me. "Then why stay?" I asked, with what I hoped was a soothing tone. Perhaps if I could switch Terry's focus from his mother to his father, I could keep his anger away from me.

Terry let up on the gas pedal as we approached a four-way stop. "Where else would I go? I couldn't leave him alone with her."

Wait, what? It baffled me.

Terry wasn't any nicer to his mom than Ken was. Putting her down was like a family sport of sorts. One they loved to practice and one that both father and son strove to win.

"You don't get it," Terry said, remorse teetering in his voice. "You haven't been here long enough. Dad holds all the cards: the business, the house, the bank accounts, everything. He controls it all. Mom and I have to finesse his ego to get anything. But Mom..."

"Your mom chose him. I can sort of understand why *she* stays around. But you? You could start a life. Somewhere else."

Terry pulled into a driveway. At the click of a clunky remote, the garage door rolled open. He drove halfway inside before shutting off the car.

"Come on," he said. "I'll show you around and then get back to the hospital."

I followed Terry into the house. My short steps barely kept up with his long strides as he hastily gave me the tour.

Bathroom, shower, towels. Check. He then pointed me to the kitchen table. "There's a map. The shop's only a couple of blocks from here," Terry said. He dug into his pocket and handed me a small key ring. "That's to the back door of the Grounds. Leave through the garage. Here's the remote. Make sure it closes. Sometimes it only half shuts."

I clumsily caught the control as he tossed it. "Got it," I said.

Terry frowned. "There's an extra coat on the rack by the front door. And an umbrella. Help yourself."

"Thanks," I whispered.

The awkwardness pressurized as silence fell. "Dad wants the store open by noon," Terry added, and then, without another word, he left.

I watched his car drive away and shut the garage door. Goosebumps covered my forearms. Quiet draped the Rockland home with eerie heaviness. It made me feel all too vulnerable.

I did not want to peel and shower. What choice did I have? If I wanted to get to work, collect a paycheck, and move on, I needed to clean up.

I hurriedly washed my hair and my body, shaking off the gravel. The hot water provoked already angry scratches. I let it linger over my injuries, purifying them.

After drying off, brushing my hair, and applying what little makeup I normally wore, I still had two hours until opening. I took a trash bag from the kitchen and stuffed my dirty clothes inside it.

In the foyer, I shoved myself into the extra winter jacket. I was thankful for the warmth. When I snagged the extra umbrella, the garage opener slipped from my hand and skittered across the tile. It landed in a small ray of sun-shaped like the beak of my all too familiar foe.

"Rats," I whispered.

The beam of light carried the Raven from the floor to the wall and from the wall to the hallway. It lighted on family portraits. Right on top of Ken's smiling face.

"No." My stomach dropped. This was one rollercoaster I could do without. "No, no, no." I pouted, walking closer to the photo.

I gingerly pulled the photo from the wall, placing the slippery remote and the store keys in a jacket pocket.

Smiling faces looked into mine: Janice and Ken and a very young Terry. The Raven sunbeam dissipated as I traced its outline on the glass. Why had it led me to this photo?

It wasn't like me to investigate. Escaping the Raven was my full-time occupation. I'd given up understanding it long ago. Still, I carried the 11 by 13 frame around with me as I looked at the other photos.

There were, of course, Terry's school snapshots. Then a few of Ken and Janice on vacation. Ken fishing with a kid in a hat. Ken and Janice on their wedding day. Janice holding baby Terry.

Her smile was so natural it made me smile in response. Ken stood behind her, bending over her and the baby. His index finger brushed the little one's plump cheek.

I squinted. That cheek didn't belong to Terry, the terror. If the room's ambiance was any sign, by the floral prints and unicorn painted on the rocker: The baby Janice was cooing at was a girl.

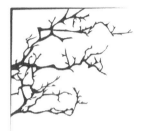

12

THE RAIN STOPPED JUST as I arrived at Rocky Grounds and Gifts. "Fantastic," I said to no one in particular.

I peeked inside the van before going into the shop. Spades still lorded over my pillow. He pretended not to see me checking in on him.

Inside Rocky Grounds, I came face to face with my previous mop bucket mess. Scrubbing the floor would be my first order of business.

Right after that, I made myself a fresh cup of coffee. Janice always made me start a shift with a mugful. She said it wasn't dipping into the profits as much as keeping her employees in touch with the clientele. If her staff didn't care for the Grounds' roasted blends, how could she expect anyone else to like them?

I hung up the jacket and the umbrella, placing a towel beneath them to catch the rainwater. Then I did a quick wipe down of the countertops. With that tidied, I hauled out an old red air popcorn popper and plugged it in.

I pulled down a bag of Guatemalan beans, scooped out enough of the tiny green seeds for two cups of coffee. Typically, after roasting, one would wait at least twelve hours before enjoying the beans. Leaving them enough time to cool, release carbon dioxide, and marinate in their natural oils. Not brew it fresh off the fire.

I liked my coffee both ways. One batch would go straight into the grinder, and the other would rest in a brown paper sack until closing. It was the best of both worlds: impatience and perseverance in separate doses of coffee.

The beans swirled into the popper. It hummed and churned as I gently shook it, ensuring all the beans received a blast of warm air. In a few moments, the beans turned from green to yellow and then yellow to warm sienna.

Thirty seconds later came my favorite part. The crisp clattering of the first crack. Musical and aromatic, the smoke curled around the red popper. I kept my eyes on the beans. A few seconds of distraction could ruin a batch. I liked my beans to flirt with second crack before I dumped them into the cooling bowl. This kept them dark without a bitter side.

Swishing them into a perforated chilled bowl, I used my other hand to unplug the popper.

A rogue bean jumped from the basket and landed on my wrist. It seared its way into the soft skin under my hoodie cuff. I flicked it off and hurried to run my hand under cool water. Fresh beans were fiery little boogers. It wasn't the first time they had burned me during my stay. It surely wouldn't be the last.

I sighed as the sting faded beneath the running faucet. I sifted silver skin from the still-hot beans- fanning them gently, to separate the chaff. It wasn't how we did things for customer batches. However, this bowlful was just for me.

I divvied up my two portions. Bagged one and brewed the other. It wasn't until the steamy water filled the French press and buried the grounds that the true coffee flavor escaped. The scent went straight to my head, whisking away the morning's drama.

If this job ended like all my previous ones, and my backward gifting led to disaster, at least I'd learned one good thing—something to carry with me, wherever life led.

I sat sipping my fresh coffee in front of the paused security monitor. Janice hadn't set it back to recording. The police hadn't been interested in seeing the footage. Once Ken explained it didn't aim at the road.

My phone photo was atrociously fuzzy—just the back of a van and a blurred license plate frame.

With a left click on the mouse, I pulled up the regular store feed. The screen flashed from the cash register to the front door and then to the back. Godzilla sat there in monochrome. Every ten seconds, the cycle repeated. Nothing noteworthy to see.

I took my coffee with me and walked out front to fill the till. The cash drawer clanked into place. There wasn't much else to do. The gift shop made only a small portion of Rocky Grounds' profits.

Most of their income came from roasted beans or green coffee orders, supplied from small family farms worldwide. Fall and winter were the two biggest money-makers for the Rocklands. Cold weather had people scampering to their coffee pots.

I had ten minutes until opening, per Ken's instructions. Just enough time to use the toilet and freshen up.

On my way back out front, I spotted the smashed package from earlier. Shoved under the desk that housed the label maker, it gave me pause. Who'd scooped it up from the road and hid it back here? Why not chuck it in the trash?

I pulled it out and carried it up to the front. Between customers, I'd catalog the damaged items. Then I could refill the order and prep a replacement box for shipping. It would make one less item on Janice's to-do list when she returned.

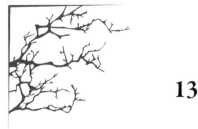

13

THE MORNING WAS BUSY. Customers came in trios. At least one of them made a purchase. All of them wanted to know if what Betty Fae had said was true. "Was Janice run down earlier that morning?"

Fellow shop owners popped by. They were the most anxious. "Did I know if it was the same group that had been threatening the block?" they asked.

I rang up Mr. Kylo from the local pharmacy to inform him that his order was ready for pick up. The short man took only minutes to show up at the Grounds. He drilled me with the same questions. Asking them in as many ways as he could think of didn't change my answer.

"Sorry," I said. "I really know nothing more about the prank calls and threats. Janice didn't talk to me about them."

Mr. Kylo clutched his Rocky Grounds purchase and a get-well card and a candle. My guess was Janice would be the future recipient of her own store's wares. He held the bag between us as he struggled to maintain eye contact with me.

"So you keep saying," he stated. "Those threats weren't coming until you arrived, you know?"

He wasn't the first person to point out the connection between my arrival with the start of the calls and letters. What could I say? I wasn't the one making them.

In fact, I'd never been around when Janice received them, either. There wasn't anything else I could add to the town narrative other than the timeline everyone else already knew.

Mr. Kylo continued shooting me side-eye as he left Rocky Grounds. Thankfully, the shop closed down from two to five on Wednesdays. Typically, we spent these hours filling orders and helping Jack load them. That wouldn't be happening today.

I'd never been so happy for a hump day. My legs dragged as I trudged out to the van, happy the rain was still resting in its cloudy bed. I triple-checked the lock on the backdoor, just in case. Though I had two hours until reopening, I would not take them all for myself. One hour was all I needed to let Spades free and make a phone call.

Spades shot from Godzilla as soon as I slid the door open. I jumped out of his way. I jostled the tattered package from one arm to the other, barely keeping it from the ground.

"You're welcome," I called after him.

Inside my van, I procrastinated. Instead of making my call right away, I cleaned and folded up my bed, tossing my grungy pillow onto the driver's seat. My bed, now a comfy couch, was the perfect place to get nosy. I pulled down the small desk slash tabletop and placed the box on it.

I popped out my electric tea kettle and plugged it in. Now that the van was running on Rocky Grounds lines, as well as drinking from the sun, I could afford a bit more luxury. I could eat my cup of noodles in peace instead of inside the shop.

I stirred the bubbling water, coaxing the rock-hard noodles to separate and soften. My thoughts dragged back to the Rockland hallway. Who was the little girl in the photos? Why hadn't anyone brought her up in conversation? Had she *died*? Is that what had caused the obvious strain between the remaining family members? If she had died, when and how?

The family memorial wall showed pictures of her with Janice and Ken as a baby. Then a handful of casual pictures of the little girl, eight or nine next to a yowling red-faced baby Terry. But that was it. Was the large age gap between the children the reason the girl was in so few photos?

All the other frames, except for the Rockland's wedding photo, starred Terry. An infant in a gown. Terry's first visit to Santa Claus. Terry dressed up for prom. None of the notable timeline photos were of the mysterious little girl.

Had she grown up only to be forgotten?

I COULD RELATE. EXCEPT it was probably for the best for me to be forgotten. There was only one person in my past I wished to see. Just once more, if only for a second. She was the reason I kept going. The reason I traveled from town to town to town.

A tiny tear rolled unsummoned down my cheek as I glanced up at the one photo that graced my tiny house. Yellowed and ragged with age, my father smiling proudly, held me on one knee and my twin sister on the other. I maintained hope that I wasn't the only one from the photo that was still breathing. Until I found Christie, I wouldn't know for sure.

I forced the tear away with the sleeve of my shirt. There wasn't time for remembering. Not with the Raven taunting me, marking its next victim. I didn't like Ken Rockland, but that didn't mean he deserved to die.

14

FINISHING LUNCH AT light speed and burning my taste buds, I hurried back into Rocky Grounds. There had to be some kind of clue to help me keep the Rocklands from disaster.

The office was the best place to begin a search. To do that, I needed to shut down the security feed. Just as Janice had done whenever Jack had visited. I'd watched over her shoulder a handful of times. Repeating her process seemed as simple as loading a roasting profile into the computer—basic steps.

The ease of entry didn't make my guilt go away. It gnawed at my stomach lining as I flipped the main recording off and faked a routine maintenance check. A pop-up flashed before me. Someone had already performed "maintenance" for the day.

It took me aback until I remembered Janice at the monitor before her encounter with the speeding van.

"Did I want to continue with maintenance?" the screen asked.

"No thanks," I spoke aloud.

One downside to being alone was that I talked to myself. A lot. When out and about, a well-placed earbud kept people from assuming I was crazy. When in for the night, Spades' company saved me from committing myself.

I closed the screen and scanned over what Janice had been doing. There was Jack, and there was Janice. They whispered to each other, but nothing overly flirtatious occurred. I watched Janice walk back to the kitchen in time to send me home. Jack paced the front of the store. He didn't approach the kitchen or the counter. His circle kept him near the shelf of coffee mugs and candles.

Janice was back in the room a moment later. She gestured toward the kitchen, explaining my departure, no doubt. Jack nodded and offered Janice his arm. She slid into her coat and linked elbows with her delivery driver. The two exited the shop without locking it and without setting the alarm.

Confused, I rewound the video. The alarm panel sat right beside the front door. In the mornings, Janice had to run from the backdoor through the kitchen to the front to punch in the four-digit code. At night, when it was just she and I, she reversed the process.

Had her distracted heart led her to forget? I wasn't sure. Shot the same night that she dumped Jack it confused me. Was dumping the correct term for ending an emotional affair?

She'd spoken of it so coolly over breakfast. Like deep feelings played no part in her choices or her desires. Maybe she'd cried herself into numbness before waffles? Or maybe she wasn't as infatuated with Jack as he was with her?

Still, forgetting to lock up and alarm your sole source of income and pride didn't seem like a Janice thing to do. Who was I to judge? I was never stuck in one place long enough to form any kind of real attachment to anything or anyone. Not anymore, anyway. Things were better that way.

But I wasn't Janice. She connected with everyone who walked into her shop. Neighborhood regular or out of towner, she treated everyone to her hospitality and smile. They never left Rocky Grounds without leaving part of their story behind.

Janice logged all their histories in her heart and talked about them as if they were family. Because to Janice, they were. At least, that's what it looked like to this wanderer.

I re-watched the feed.

If she'd left the door unlocked, that would explain the vandals' ease of access. They didn't need to break anything to get inside Rocky Grounds. Just turn the handle and go in.

For vandals, they hadn't done all that much damage. Dumping shelves and drawers were relatively minor. They could've robbed the place clean. The register. The safe. Even the neatly stacked outbound delivery would have been excellent items to pilfer. Especially without an alarm buzzing above them. Why hadn't they seized the opportunity?

Since there was so minor damage, Janice didn't alert the police to the break-in even after the near-miss, possibly by the same vandals coming back with a car large enough to carry more loot.

It confused me then. Now, it worried me. Maybe she felt it was her fault for leaving the place unlocked.

I scrolled through the footage, hoping to find the break-in on black and white. It never came. Only Janice came in through the front, finding the wreckage and me running around the back to let my cat out.

Janice walked inside, stepped over the damage, and went straight back to the kitchen. Before unlocking the back for me, she swung into the office. She riffled through the tossed papers, opened the safe, pulled out a manila envelope, and locked the safe back up.

I hadn't noticed an envelope in her hand when she let me in. I wasn't paying attention. After seeing Janice's panic-laden expression, I'd followed her swiftly to the front.

She hadn't had the envelope on her when the truck plowed her down. Where was it? And why was it so important for her to retrieve it?

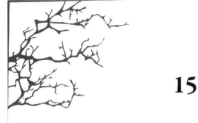

15

THE FRONT DOOR OF THE shop opened, and I launched from my position at the security monitor. Right into Janice.

She smirked. "What are you up to?"

Ken followed her into the kitchen. He smiled a rarity. "Looks great in here."

I almost choked. Was that a kind word from Mr. Rockland? Maybe almost losing his wife had him scared straight? Just in time to die. I shivered.

No, no. I thought. *It doesn't have to end that way. There can be happy endings.*

As if to knock me back into my senses, Ken's shadow flapped at me in winged fashion. No other clues followed. I didn't know how to help him or his wife.

Janice put a gauze-wrapped hand on my shoulder. "Penny, sweetie, I'm alright." She sounded like a mother coaxing her child to sleep. The false sense of safety was not what I was buying. I couldn't. I knew better.

I offered Janice my most reassuring smile. Her returning expression brimmed with questions. Her eyebrow lifted as her focus flickered to the security monitor.

"Ken," she said.

Ken was right there, waiting for her next words. Attentive and helpful. Odd how creepy sweetness can be when it comes from an unexpected source.

"What do you need?"

"Penny has everything handled here." Janice didn't look at her husband. Her glances rotated between the monitor and me. "Why don't you get the car and pull it up front? We'll ask Terry to come down and help with the evening shift. There's no reason for us to stay."

"Really?" Ken asked, overjoyed. "One day of rest won't kill you, just like the doctor said." He planted a tender smooch on the top of Janice's hair and hurried to comply with her wishes.

Who was this new Ken?

"Looking for the intruders?" Janice asked, sidling up next to me. She placed her hand over mine and scrolled the screen back to its regular rotation.

"Maybe there was something the police missed. Something that might help us find who hurt you," I offered.

"So sweet," Janice said. She backed away slowly. "But unnecessary. Let's forget about it. Okay?" With that, Janice shut the monitor off completely. Then patted my shoulder one more time. "It's better that way," she said. "There's no use stirring up the bees if there's still honey in the pot."

I watched her leave the kitchen, dumbfounded. Maybe she feared worse retaliation if she turned over the security feed. Maybe she was on pain meds.

Little did she know there was no feed to turn over to the police. As I discovered, moments before she and Ken arrived. Someone erased it. Two hours had vanished entirely.

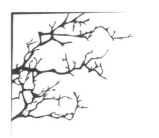

16

I WASN'T ABOUT TO GIVE up. However, there was little I could do without help. Short from telling Janice and Ken about my creepy "gift," I couldn't deter them or force them to stay indoors, locked safely away.

The last time I'd told a friend about my suspicions, minus the glimpses of the future, they'd done the kindest thing they believed possible. They tried to have me declared insane.

I didn't hold a grudge. What would I do if some chubby teenager I'd just met told me I was about to die? If the Raven hadn't succeeded, I might have permanent reservations at Watson's Wellbeing Clinic. Since the Raven was victorious, they merely chased me out of town in a pitchfork mob fashion.

I barely escaped. Rumor had it there were still a few lingering naysayers who were watching for me to return. Waiting to exact their revenge on the runaway, they'd declared a witch.

A witch? Ha. I didn't hold any power over what was happening to me. I was at the Raven's call, just as its victims were.

For some unknown reason, he liked to flaunt his prey before me and make my life miserable. There was no summoning him or sending him away. The Raven just was. I was constantly wary of its appearance. And all my other glimpses.

I let the front bell settle before peeking out the front window. The Rocklands had zoomed away, presumably to rest and recover at home.

I left the door locked and hurried to the kitchen. I had a few pounds of green beans to roast and a computer to hack. Not that I knew how to hack anything. That wouldn't stop me from trying. I snickered.

I set the roaster profile, poured in the Costa Rican beans, and monitored the laptop controlling the roaster. The computer was as precise as possible, but after Terry's incident with the burned batch, I was worried. I watched the graph light up as the fan speed and temperature rose and fell at the pre-set times.

Meanwhile, I dug around in the Rocky Grounds security computer.

Janice hadn't completely shut down the device, only the feed. As of now, the cameras were like expensive yard signs pretending that security was live and on-call.

I minimized the blackened feed and rummaged through the files. Three main folders stood out. Rocky Grounds Reports, Rocky Grounds Profiles, and Rocky Grounds Marketing. There was nothing suspicious about any of those. A quick click and shuffle showed only the files one would expect under such titles. Lots of spreadsheets and invoices. None of them are big enough reasons to off someone.

Then again, murderers never made sense. At least in my experience. And though the Raven's appearance could mean any mode of expiration, more often than not, it meant murder.

There were a lot of reasons to dislike Ken. At least to the naked eye. He was rude and borderline vulgar. He seemed to hate his wife and despise his son. The list of annoyances and irritating behaviors was long and varied. None were a good enough reason to kill him.

Then, just before opening, I remembered the manila envelope. I risked leaving a digital imprint to reopen the security feed and tailed Janice from the time she'd gone into the office to the moment I'd returned to her sitting in front of the monitor.

She disappeared only once. To unlock the back door for me. There wasn't a lot over there to see, other than the mop bucket and cleaning supplies.

With three minutes to spare, I moved aside a container of kitchen cleaner and piles of clean rags. I lifted a box of laundry soap but nearly chucked it across the room. The usually heaving box was lighter than a loaf of bread. I struggled not to drop it in my over-exuberant hoist.

I went to toss it in the garbage when a needling in my chest told me to give it a double glance. Inside was a manila envelope. The same one Janice cradled in the security feed. Curved but not bent, it hid inside the soap-scented cardboard.

I put it in my backpack. I shoved my bag onto the shelf Janice had assigned for it. Then I replaced the empty box, just in case. There was no other reason than a dirty secret to hide documents in an empty detergent box. I couldn't risk someone coming around to retrieve the envelope before I'd check it out.

Work came first. There were more nosy customers hanging around outside. I'd have to wait until after the store closed for the night.

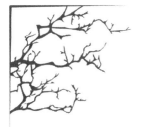

17

THE REST OF THE WORKDAY dragged on. The manila envelope was never far from my mind. Neither was the clock's constant clicking, counting down the minutes Ken had left to live. My worries over Janice hadn't fully subsided, either.

Historically, the Raven selected only one victim at a time. If thwarted, all bets were off, as I'd learned just a month earlier. That time, saving one victim led to another being snatched, plus more collateral damage than any small town gossip could handle.

I could only hope Ken was now the primary target. The Raven in his picture at his home and his shadow at the shop solidified my concerns. It hadn't reappeared with Janice when she showed up damaged and disconnected from her early encounter with the bird.

Sunset had settled over the main square before Terry walked through the front door and straight into the kitchen. He winked at me as he passed, but said nothing.

I knew he was supposed to take over for me in the front so I could finish up orders in the back. That didn't mean I'd expected him to show.

He strolled back into the front with a fresh register in hand. "Go ahead," he said, nodding toward the kitchen. "Stick your register in the safe and take your dinner break."

My mouth dropped. "You sure?"

"Of course, I'm sure." Terry slid out my cash drawer and shoved it at me. "Now get. I'll see you in an hour."

I held the drawer, still perplexed. "An hour?"

"Geez." Terry huffed. "What do you think I am? A monster? You've been here all day alone. I think a longer break is more than due you. Now beat it!"

"Thanks," I said. Terry waved me away as he entered his employee id into the register.

I hustled to obey, eager to rip open a specific envelope.

RAIN TINKLED ON THE roof of the van. The electric heater hummed happily, keeping Spades and I cozy. I didn't have the energy to eat. Exhausted from the early morning, near accident, and the long work hours, I could only drum up enough gusto to peel open a string cheese. I nibbled it before slowly opening the envelope.

Unsure what to expect, I came face to face with two documents. Or scanned copies of documents, to be exact. Two nearly identical wills were signed by Kenneth J. Rockland. I slumped back against my futon couch. Spades curled around my feet.

Peeking inside the envelope, I found a flash drive wearing a plastic green and white fob. I took a picture of each document and the logo on the fob with my cell before I skimmed each will for differences. Speed kept me from picking up anything outstanding on the first pass.

The last thing I wanted was for Ken or Terry to find me hoarding their personal papers. If Janice had been so concerned as to hide them, something inside of them must be important. Something she needed out of Ken's reach. Out of respect for her, I needed to do the same.

After a second pass, with weary eyes, I gave up on the lawyer's speech and opted to plug the flash drive into my laptop. Folders marked by date lined up neatly on my screen.

I clicked the first one. Photos. Ken and a woman in the distance. Ken and a woman eating lunch. Ken and a woman embracing. I frowned.

He really *had* given up on his marriage to the loyal Janice? If she knew this and had the folder in her possession, then why did she stick around? Why did she end things with Jack? Wouldn't this information free her to be with him? After finding out what happened to his missing wife, of course.

I opened another folder. More pictures of the same pair. All at a distance. Close enough for me to make out Ken because I knew him and was used to seeing him. None of them were near enough to make out the woman. Only that she was young and had brown hair. She was always wearing sunglasses in every photo, no matter the weather or lack of sunshine.

I plugged the dates, aligning with each folder into the computer. Each had been on a Wednesday afternoon. Ken's normal fishing day.

Sure, he goes fishing, but not for trout, I thought.

I didn't know what else to do with the information I had. There was so little time. The store would close before I could gather any other clues or alert Ken and make sure Janice didn't get caught in the crossfire. The Raven slated someone to die. If I ticked him off enough, that someone might be me.

I needed help. There was only one place I could get it. But making the call made my palms sweat and my heart flip. "What am I doing?"

Spades answered me with a long stretch and a flick of his white-tipped tail. He then turned his back on me before launching from my lap and squeezing out of the passenger window.

"Some pal you are," I scoffed at my feline friend.

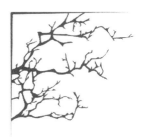

18

CRADLING MY PHONE BETWEEN my ear and shoulder, I dialed the only person I believed could help me help Janice. Though it meant I was embracing insanity. While I listened to the other end ring, I sliced open the smashed box from the morning.

After the first delicate tug on the packing tape, the entire bundle collapsed. I sifted through the cardboard to find nothing. Nothing other than packing paper. I shoved the paper aside, pushed it back, shook it, and looked under it. Nothing. But Janice had been so desperate to make sure it made the morning's delivery.

"Why would someone mail an empty box?"

"I'm sorry, what? Penny? Is that you?" Scrubb answered T.C.'s work cell.

"Yes, yes, it's Penny."

"T.C. isn't here," Scrubb said.

"That's fine. Fine," I responded. "It's you I need, anyway."

"Really? Okay."

"T.C. said once that you're good with computers. How good?"

Scrubb chuckled. "Good."

"The girl from Jurassic Park, good?"

"Better." He laughed. "What do you need?"

I detailed my thoughts on the mysterious family member on the Rocklands' wall. Then sent Scrubb my fuzzy text of the wheeled weapon that had nearly smashed Janice.

"That's all you got?" Scrubb asked. "It won't be easy. Anything else?"

I made a hasty choice and forwarded all my document pictures and the photo files to Scrubb. "Do you think you can figure this stuff out for me? It's in legalese, and I'm beyond tired."

"T.C. is great with boring documents," Scrubb pronounced. "I'll work on the pictures. See if we can get a better close-up."

"I'm sure it's simple for someone with your skills and connections. You and T.C. hunt people all the time."

Scrubb corrected me, "We hunt the *truth*, not people. What's this last picture? The green one?"

"It's the flash drive fob. Probably the company who took the photos. At least that's my guess."

"I'd say it's a good one." I could hear Scrubb clicking away on his keyboard. He was already digging into the clues for me.

A breath I'd been holding since breakfast released. I wasn't alone in this., for once. I'd have to wait to see if that was a good thing or a bad thing.

"I've got to head to work and put these things back." I paused, hesitant to ask what had to be asked. "Scrubb, do you believe me? About my glimpses, I mean?"

A poignant pause broke Scrubb's typing stride. "I'm not sure. I've definitely seen weirder things."

His honesty hurt and healed at the same time. At least I could trust him not to pander to my every whim. If we became any better acquainted, friends even, Scrubb was the sort of guy who'd stick by me and tell it like it was. I appreciated his candor. In a world of crazy, a real person was hard to find.

"I'll tell you this." Scrubb interrupted my thoughts. "T.C. believes you one hundred percent and then some."

There was a hint of a threat lingering in this declaration. A sort of "hurt him, and I'll hurt you" promise. He must've witnessed T.C. being hurt before. Badly.

"Thanks," was all I could say.

"Be careful, Penny."

"Sure," I said. "When do you think you'll know something?"

"Shouldn't take too long," Scrubb answered. "I'll text you. Is there anything you'd like me to tell T.C.?"

Um, no, I thought. I wouldn't be calling, except I needed help. This was too much for me to handle on my own in the next eighteen hours.

"Um, no," I said.

"Got it. Mum's the word." Scrubb signed off just as Spades leaped back into the van.

The black cat with a white spade on his neck curled up on my lap, apparently forgiving me for the moment. I gave his back a quick scratch when a loud crash stole the scene.

19

SECURING JANICE'S HIDDEN envelope and its contents within my borrowed jacket, I locked Spades in the van and hurried to see what was happening. With a hand to the doorknob, I paused. If something sinister was afoot, charging into the center of the crisis would benefit no one. Least of all, me.

I shoved my ear against the backdoor and listened. Nothing but scuffling and an electric hum echoed from inside the shop. If I went around the front, they could catch me with the envelope. If I walked in the back, they could sweep me up in whatever drama was occurring inside.

I scooted around the side of the shop toward Main Street. Maybe I could manage a peek in without being spotted.

The noise grew louder around the front of the building. Just as I was about to look, two people in hooded coats rushed from the shop and down the street. I watched them pile into a white van on the far end of the road and speed away. A van that looked a lot like the one I'd seen earlier that day.

My head ached at the thought of more traumas. I waited for a tick, expecting Terry to come charging out of the shop, chasing the hooligans. Then I realized he might not be able to. Not if someone hurt him. I pulled my cell phone out and called emergency services.

Inside the shop, the vandals had done a much better job wrecking the place than they had done earlier. Broken glass shimmered beneath brown coffee beans. The cash register was upside down. It scattered coins in its wake.

A low moaning came from under the greeting card rack. Terry's shoes stuck out amongst the belated birthday section. I struggled to upright the shelf. Terry was groggy from his attack.

"They just busted in. Screaming. Tossing things," he muttered, more to himself than to me. Leaning against the wall, Terry's eyes didn't connect with mine. They flickered wildly around the room.

"I've called for help," I told him. "It's on the way."

"But, but," Terry stammered. "Oh my gosh, Dad."

"Dad?"

"He stopped by to do a cash drop. He was in the back by the safe."

My stomach flipped. There was more than one reason I didn't want Mr. Rockland at the store at that moment. I ran to the back, stumbling over my laces, and skittered across the slick floor. Smack into the limp body of my boss.

Stunned, it took me longer than it should have to yank Ken's head from the mop basin. There was no way he'd accidentally fallen into the water. Someone had to force his head in there. His lips were light blue, but his eyes weren't bulging.

I laid him on his back and shouted to Terry. "Get help! Now!"

Terry's voice was more of a rattled whine than an acknowledgment.

In the past, I was a lifeguard at a community pool. In hindsight, it was a terrible choice of a profession for someone with my abnormalities. But it had taught me CPR, a skill one could always use. I kept up my training with yearly refresher courses, usually sponsored by a small-town library or elementary school.

I was working on Ken before my brain registered my motions. Autopilot was a great perk for the hyper-paranoid. It meant I always had an escape plan hatching and worst-case scenarios were cakewalks.

It only took a few rounds of breath and compressions for Ken to gag and breathe for himself.

I fell back onto my rear. Television shows did absolutely no justice to the price one paid to rescue another person. It wore out every part of you. Body, mind, spirit instantly zapped. My thighs and shoulders burned.

With Ken slowly growing more aware of his surroundings, I should've been high on gratitude. But I had nothing left. Depleted, I watched as Terry casually checked on his father until the paramedics arrived.

"Two in one day," the blond paramedic told his partner.

Paramedic number two flashed a strange look of implication at me. "Good thing she's been here to save them. Both."

From his lowered stretcher, Ken reached out and grabbed my hand. "That's my Lucky Penny," he croaked before they lifted him for his trek to the ambulance.

"Isn't she just?" Terry said, arms folded against his chest. His eyes narrowed as he cataloged my presence. Almost with x-ray precision, he bore his thoughts into my gut. Terry blamed me. He suspected my part in these two near disasters.

As the medics brushed past him, carting his father away, a black shadow crept from beneath his feet. The bird was back- still marking Mr. Rockland.

The overhead music buffered. It went to commercials and then played *Lyin' Eyes* by the Eagles- A staple on every truck stop radio I'd ever encountered.

I thought it over for a moment. No revelations unraveled, other than Janice's nearly romantic fling with Jack. Was her jilted almost lover behind the vandalism? Maybe even the attempted murders?

I shivered beneath Terry's inquisitive look. He was inspecting me. For what? Weakness? Motive? Was Terry worried I was the one who'd caused each trauma? Or was he ticked that I'd stopped his attempts to free himself of his parents?

I wasn't sure. One thing was obvious. Terry was less than overwhelmed by the murder attempt on his father's life. Even less than he'd been when his mother was run down.

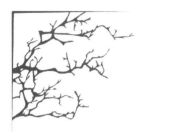

20

JANICE DIDN'T COME down to the shop. Terry said she drove straight to the hospital to check on her husband. Maybe they could find common ground in their near-death experiences? Grow a new and healthier relationship? I doubted it, especially if Terry had anything to say about it.

He stayed at the shop to talk with the police, who were more than a little baffled by two occurrences in the same location on the same day. I squirmed under their interrogations. There wasn't much I could say. Revealing the morning's vandalism against Janice's wishes only frustrated them. It wouldn't be long before they added up the coincidences and ran my name through a database somewhere.

The police always did. It made sense. All they found was my sad past: dead parents and foster families. Deaths followed by more deaths. A small smattering of nonfatal disasters. Then me, right in the center of the mess. Without motive or opportunity, and with absolutely no binding evidence, I was always let go.

Sometimes I wondered if prison would be better. But I quickly reminded myself that the Raven was no respecter of persons or stations in life. A densely packed population of a jail or an insane asylum, if I was lucky, offered more carrion for him to feed upon. Considering that revelation, I kept fighting for and maintaining my innocence.

I didn't kill anyone. I would never lay a hand on them. Did that make me innocent? Or an accomplice after the fact? It didn't matter. For now, I needed to ride out the next few hours until the police told me I was free to leave. Then I would unplug Godzilla and head on to another town. By then, T.C.'s second payment should've hit my bank, and I'd have enough money to make it through winter. With any luck, that is.

Officer Tyler sat on the kitchen island. I frowned. I'd have to bleach the room, yet again. Terry swayed in the rolling office chair.

"Your dad didn't have any enemies? Anyone wanting to take over his store or business?" he asked, looking over the top of his spectacles.

"Dad?" Terry shook his head. "You've met him, right?"

The officer laughed. "Yes."

"Then you know. He was a pain. *Is* a pain."

The officer chuckled. I blanched. Usually, relatives of victims have a difficult time talking about the deceased in the past tense. Terry did it the other way around. It was unsettling. Officer Tyler did not seem to notice. I wondered why.

"Remember when he came to our senior poker night and pitched a fit over the trash?" Officer Tyler recalled.

That explained it. Officer Tyler and Terry were once classmates.

Terry reddened. He remembered the event and was still angry about it. "Sure. I mean, how could I forget? Donna Winsome broke up with me right after that. She said she didn't want to get roped into a family with a dad like that at the helm." Terry picked at his nails while he replayed the embarrassment in his mind.

"Little did she know, right?" Officer Tyler said.

"What does that mean?" I asked, forgetting I'd decided to stay invisible.

Officer Tyler glared at me. "You've met Janice. She is in charge of that relationship."

Terry changed the subject. "Back to your questions. Other than the phone calls that every other merchant on Main Street has been getting, I can't think of anyone who'd want this lousy shop. Besides Mom and me."

"Hmm?" Officer Tyler said, shaking off his casual demeanor. He turned his attention to me. I shrunk back against the countertop.

"Why didn't Mrs. Rockland call the police this morning?"

I swallowed. This would be the third time I answered that question. I wished Officer Tyler would write things down. He seemed to rely only on his charming conversational skills to draw out information on a whim. It wasn't a great technique for him.

"She didn't want to cause a fuss and thus insight more anger from the vandals. Nothing was broken. Nothing was taken. Unlike this evening."

"You're sure there's no video of it?"

Terry answered for me, "Nope. The cameras weren't working."

I blinked. Yes, they were. But someone had scrambled the tape.

Janice said that Terry and Ken never noticed when she'd deleted the video of her and Jack. Maybe she'd told them the system was glitching during those times.

"Are they working now?"

Terry answered again. "Mom shut them down. She said they were recalibrating."

Surely, Terry couldn't be that dim. He was closer to my age than either Ken or Janice. He had to know more about computers than his mom did. It was an accepted generational gap. Technology awareness was continually growing, and so the younger folks got the most up-to-date training. Whereas their parents, unless they purposefully sought higher learning, ate their virtual dust.

Terry knew more than Janice. I knew more than Terry. Though only a year younger than me, Scrubb knew more than I did. Thank goodness, I'd be hearing from him soon.

"Well, they smashed things up this time. Was there anything specific that they seemed to be after?"

In reflex, my eyes shot to the soap shelf. Sure enough, the box of soap flakes was missing. I didn't allow my gaze to linger in case Officer Tyler read too much from it.

Returning my attention to the conversation, I caught sight of two things in my peripherals. One was the manila envelope sitting on the wet floor next to the mop bucket. It must've fallen from my jacket as I worked chest compressions on Ken. The second was that Terry had spotted the envelope, and he'd also recognized my distress at seeing it there.

21

I WAS BEYOND GRATEFUL when, after another hour of questions, Officer Tyler watched as Terry locked the store and then walked me to my van. Terry lingered at the corner of the shop. I wondered if he was planning to reopen when his friend wasn't looking. Then the officer set out a security patrol for the street.

"No need to risk a third break-in," he joked. "That and the rest of Main Street is in a state of panic. Wondering if they'll be next."

I slid the van's door closed. It wasn't the first time I wished Godzilla really was a radioactive dinosaur from thor at least a house with sturdier walls and locks. I was more than a little vulnerable in my glorified tin can of a home.

The winter sun had set a long time ago. A fresh smattering of rain drummed along the roof. Normally, the sound was relaxing. Not when I was listening for approaching vandals or murderers. It only amplified my paranoia.

Which is why it surprised me when I woke from a sitting sleep. Curled around my knees, I'd cried myself into a paralyzed stupor. From the time on my phone, it had only been ten minutes from when I'd last checked for Scrubb's call. Just enough rest to make me feel even more tired than I already was.

When the phone rang, I tossed it across the van. Smacking an angry Spades on the tail, it sailed out of reach and clattered to the ground. Spades swiped at it, turning on the speaker.

"Penny?" T.C.'s voice echoed around the van. "Penny, are you okay?"

"Hold on," I croaked, still too sleepy to make my voice cooperate. I crawled to it. "I dropped my phone."

Drool moistened my cheek. I wiped it away with the sleeve of my sweater before placing the cell to my ear. Spades hissed at me.

"Just a second," I said as I hurried to roll down the front window. Manually cranking the window down, watching Spades pout his way into the rain, and manually cranking it back up did not produce the most ladylike of noises.

"Sorry about that." I hoped T.C. wasn't laughing at me.

"No worries," his voice remained ever steady and kind. Which, of course, made me highly suspicious of it.

I shook away my personal issues and settled back on the couch. But I did not relax. Spades would yowl to come back inside in no time. He was a cat, and water was not his favorite element. Mad at me or not, he'd be wanting in sooner than later.

"Okay, I'm here," I puffed.

"Scrubb said you called?"

My stomach twisted. I wished Scrubb hadn't told T.C. about my call.

Scrubb was more like me. Closer in age. Used to being misunderstood. Friendly, but not overly so. But T.C., T.C. made little sense to me. Sure, he pursued the semi-paranormal for his podcasts. Over the last few months, he'd taken on fewer and fewer fresh cases to investigate mine. Why? What did he hope to find out? How did he think I could help him?

"Yes," I said. "I'm having issues with my current employers. He's looking into some things for me." I stayed as vague as possible.

T.C.'s frown was audible. My distrust hurt him—another reason to question his motives.

"He told me," he said, in his slight British accent. 'We've been diving into your case. Let me put you on speaker, and he can tell you what we found."

A beep later, Scrubb echoed through the line. "Hey, Penny," he said.

I pictured him sitting near T.C., at his own desk. Though I'd never visited their studio, I imagined it was well stocked and organized. Maybe it was T.C.'s faint accent that gave me the impression of posh and propriety. Perhaps it was his age. At least seven years older than Scrubb and I, T.C. had an awkward professor of ancient tomes' aesthetic. His signature gray glasses, amplified by his lanky frame, supported my theories.

Truth be told, I didn't know enough about the man to sum him up. There were moments, brief as they were, that he reminded me of my father. That was enough of a red flag to keep me at arm's length.

"What's the scoop?"

"First off, the fob belongs to a private investigator from the city. I talked to him, but of course, he didn't tell me anything I hadn't already figured out." I caught the pout in Scrubb's voice.

"Like who hired him?" I asked.

"Oh, that we figure out ourselves?" T.C. chuckled. "It's not who you'd think."

"Janice?"

"Nope. Terrance Rockland," Scrubb announced.

Terry? I thought. Surprised, the man had enough gumption to do something that drastic for himself. I figured he luxuriated in his benefiting bystander persona. One to reap the rewards without doing an iota of the work. "That's interesting. Was he trailing Ken for signs of infidelity? For his mother, perhaps?"

"It doesn't appear so," Scrubb said. His voice was closer to the speaker. He must've moved over to T.C.'s side of the room.

"Then what are those photos?"

Scrubb cleared his throat. "They're Ken, sure enough. And he's with a Miss Pearl Rockland."

"Don't tell me," I shouted, scaring the recently returned Spades. He snarled and turned his back toward me. It had not been the greatest of days for my renegade cat and me. "His daughter."

"Bingo," Scrubb announced. "How did you know?"

"I spotted a few family photos with a girl I'd never met in them. She looked about eight years older than Terry."

"Exactly," Scrubb said. "Pearl is thirty-two."

I sighed. It was nice to know she was alive. From her sudden photographic absence, I guessed she had passed away. I was happy she hadn't. That still didn't explain the weirdness of a missing family member in most of their iconic shots.

"Why would Terry need to hunt her down?" I asked. "She's his sister. Wouldn't they still be in contact?"

"You'd think so, right?" T.C. said.

Scrubb added, "She's actually Terry's half-sister. At eleven, they sent her to live with her mother. She rarely came back to the Rocklands. Then, from what we've been able to scrounge when Pearl was about seventeen, she was in a horrible accident."

"But she's still alive?"

"Yes," Scrubb said. "It took her almost a year to get out of a rehab hospital."

"Just when she'd be heading off to college or to start a life of her own," I mourned aloud for Pearl's pain.

"That might have been the point," T.C. interjected.

Thunder shook Godzilla. I squealed, already tense from the day and jumpy beyond sense. This time, Spades was so livid he scratched the seats. I was turning my feline friend into a neurotic mess.

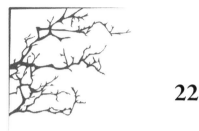

22

"SORRY ABOUT THAT," I hollered to my speaker as I shut the wind out of my tiny home on wheels. Spades was livid with me if he would risk the weather over the cozy van. "Explain what you mean by plan," I demanded.

T.C. took over the conversation. "Let's start with the wills. One appears to be authentic. Someone has tampered with the other. Unless Mr. Rockland did the tampering and is planning to shoot it past his legal counsel, I don't see how it would stand in court. One never can tell. It could be a rough draft. It looks newer than the other, but both documents are only copies of the originals. There's no telling which one is the real one."

"So, someone messed with them. Why?" I draped my electric blanket over my legs and plugged it in. Letting Spades free had let in just enough cold air to send shivers up my shins.

"To change who benefits. Why else? Basically, in one document, Terry and Pearl split Ken's cash and the store. In the other, Janice gets the house and the cash with the stipulation that she cares for Pearl. Terry gets the store, providing he moves out of his mother's house."

I frowned. Ken was frequently complaining about Terry's apron string addiction. I didn't see entirely how one mattered more than the other. Except that Janice is cut out of one.

Could that make Janice mad enough to kill Ken? I guess crazier things had happened. It didn't explain the vandals or Janice's chicken fight with the mysterious van. "How would that amount to Terry devising an evil plan? To what? Find his sister?"

"We don't think he was trying just to find his sister," Scrubb said.

"You think he was trying to kill her?" I asked. The hairs on my neck rose and not because of the chill.

"We don't want to jump to any conclusions, but with her out of the way, if Janice and Ken die, he gets all of Ken's assets," Scrubb added.

"If only Ken dies, it leaves Janice to fend for herself," T.C. chimed in. "In both copies, he's adamant that Terry move out on his own."

"Hold on. Back that up." I rubbed my temples.

Had Terry run down his own mother? Surely he wouldn't be stupid enough to kill Ken. Not for the store and cash. By the books, the store did well but not set one-up-for-life well. Judging by their home decor, I doubted Ken had the money to make anyone justify murder.

"In will number one," T.C. said. "If Ken dies, Janice gets everything. In the second, Terry and Pearl do. But if Janice were to die, then Terry would be in charge of all the assets."

"What assets?" Struggling to keep the frustration out of my tone, I hungered for more information. Who was I working for? "The store barely makes anything. It's not like anyone would roll in gold coins after inheriting all the Rockland estate. Let alone half of it."

Scrubb giggled. "Do you want to tell her, or should I?"

T.C.'s voice echoed Scrubb's cheer. "Go for it, my young apprentice."

"I hate when you call me that," Scrubb sneered playfully. "Ken is loaded. I mean, like super-rich. Why he holes up in a small town, running a small business, is beyond me."

"For the tax breaks," T.C. commented.

"He's that rich," Scrubb said. "Getting only the store would be the equivalent of inheriting your grandmother's scarf collection while all your cousins get new houses. It's a snub."

"A snub at who? Janice? Terry?"

T.C.'s voice deepened. "That's where things get tangled."

"Did Pearl know? She has the most to lose and the most to gain. At least one of them knows about these wills. If not, both of them. Terry makes sense. Why would he hunt down his sister just to rob her of her inheritance? Plus, Ken knew where she was. Why not just ask him?"

"There's the sticky bit," T. C. said.

"Sticky, how?"

Scrubb's voice crackled as someone on his side shifted papers. "The accident we found."

"Yes?"

"Pearl has healed, but not completely. The accident left her blind."

"Huh? What does that have to do with it?"

T.C. and Scrubb battled over what to say next. Phone calls got tricky when dealing with such intense discussion I couldn't take waiting for the information. It was making me nuts. After a quick check of my face in the rearview mirror, I hit the video call button.

"She's videoing us," T.C. said, confused.

"Hit the button, man," Scrubb said.

In a moment, I was staring up T.C.'s nostrils as Scrubb adjusted their phone. I set mine on my small desk slash table. When the bustling settled, I was face to screen with T.C., in his usual state of professorial disarray. Scrubb was sitting casually next to him in a high-backed rolling chair.

I still couldn't believe I was stooping to such a level. But what else could I do? Standing by would only envelop me in guilt. Even if no one else in the world knew about my glimpses, I did. That was enough. I'd stood by too many times before. Now was the time to stand up to the bird. Time to fight back.

That meant staring down my pseudo-stalker and his assistant. At least they were towns away. Even though I knew they'd looked up my location, as soon as I'd spilled the beans about the Rocklands, they were too far away to take me by surprise especially, if they were sitting pretty in their studio.

"That's better," I said, still unsure if it really was.

T.C. adjusted his glasses and shot his awkward, toothy smile at me. His dark eyes crossed the wireless and linked with mine. I shuttered. It wasn't wholly unpleasant. In fact, I could easily see myself getting too comfy staring back into those eyes. However, in the current situation, they were all too distracting.

My pulse spiked as I pried my eyes from his and convinced myself to look at Scrubb. His young face frowned at me. He'd seen my momentary lapse of shielding. I forced myself to smile. Scrubb nodded. He wouldn't let on.

"Okay, let's start this again," Scrubb said, shaking both T.C. and me back to the present. "Pearl's seventeen and run over."

"Run over? Like Janice, run over?"

Scrubb nodded. "Exactly. They never caught the driver. Except we have a partial license plate for that car. I'll text it to you." Scrubb instantly pulled out his phone. His thumbs went flying, and seconds later, my phone alerted me to his message.

"Got it," I said. "After the accident, Pearl went to rehab. Terry was what? Ten?"

"Exactly," T.C. said. "They hadn't lived as a family for years."

"Right, I'm tracking."

"Good," Scrubb said. "When Pearl gets out of rehab, Ken hires tutors and specialists to help her adjust to life without sight."

"Those are not cheap," T.C. added. "I speak from experience."

I felt him staring at me. I forced my eyes to stay loose and rotate between the speakers, like a driver, glancing from mirror to gauges to the road and back around, I kept oscillating my attention. It was exhausting and meant Scrubb had to repeat himself far too many times.

"Then, last year, Pearl's mom died. That's when they drafted will number one," he read from a sheet in front of him. "Ken moved her to a community for the blind. They helped her get a job and acclimate to life on her own. She's doing well for herself."

"That explains why Ken wants the bulk of the money to go to her. She's going to need it more than Terry," I said.

"Now, who did you say you caught a glimpse on?" T.C. asked so casually, as if my peeks behind death's curtain were everyday occurrences.

I shuddered. "This morning, Janice."

"You saw more than one?" T.C.'s face held a heightened glimmer of interest. We were entering his territory now. The weird and semi-paranormal, as he called it.

"Yes." I paused, scouting for the right words. "But after her accident, it switched to Ken."

"Because you saved her?"

I shrugged. If I understood the Raven, I wouldn't have to live my life trying to dodge it. At least, that was my hope. And one of my biggest reasons for allowing T.C. a ringside seat to my sideshow.

"Is that normal?" Scrubb asked.

"Is any of this normal?" I replied.

After a long pause, T.C. stated in flat tones, "We have two victims. They named both on the will. Each one's death directly affects the outcome of the will. We have two beneficiaries. One is blind and living an hour away. Hardly capable of driving a van to smash her stepmother. And the other lives and works with the victims."

"Is it that clear to you?" I asked.

It was plausible. Terry Rockland was trying to kill his parents. The boys offered little reassurance.

"What exactly am I supposed to do? I have no actual evidence. Just hunches. Hunches that make me look even more involved in the whole mess than I really am." I ran a hand through my hair.

T.C.'s left eyebrow spiked. He was suddenly fidgety. Scrubb's worried expression did nothing to lift my spirits. We all knew what I was going to do. I was going to confront the bad guy in my haphazard fashion. I was going to have a face-to-face with Terry Rockland and a toe-to-toe with the Raven. Plus, I was going to do it alone.

"We can be there in four hours," Scrubb said. T.C.'s Adam's apple bobbed as he repeatedly swallowed like he was trying to keep his cool.

"Four hours will be too late," I whispered. "If I'm going to save Janice and Ken, I have to do it tonight."

"Be safe, kid," Scrubb said.

T.C. lifted a finger to the screen as if he was trying to touch my face. "We'll be praying."

I swallowed back fearful hot tears and struggled to grin with confidence. I could tell by their mirrored half-smiles we were all faking it.

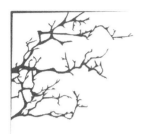

23

NORMALLY, I RUN IN the other direction in a dangerous situation- screeching and stumbling as I go. Two things compelled me to stick around town. Saving my friend Janice Rockland, and if possible, her husband, and the minor fact that I plugged my van into her gift shop.

Though it was still raining, I wrapped up in my borrowed jacket and used my borrowed umbrella to trudge back to the Rockland's house. I wasn't sure what I would find there. At least, if things went wrong, for once, I'd have people who knew where to look for my body. That thought sent waves of sickness swirling about my stomach.

I hurried along, avoiding puddles before my courage wore thin. My hands trembled as I rang the bell, hiding beneath the stoop and out of the rain. Clattering sounds echoed from within, shattering and screeching. I panicked. Fists to the wood, I knocked and rang ferociously until I heard footsteps coming to answer.

Terry swung the door wide. His red-rimmed eyes examined me with curiosity. "What are you doing here?" he asked, leaving me just enough room to push past him and into the foyer.

Sometimes having a wide rear was a blessing. It meant more weight to shove people aside. I charged down the hallway, peeping into every room. "Janice?" I called. "Janice, where are you?"

I kept darting my attention back to where I'd last seen Terry. I couldn't let him sneak up on me. Clobber me like he had his father. At the last bedroom door, I plunged into the room, ripping open closets. Janice wasn't there.

I hurried to the garage, right past Terry. Skidding in my wet sneakers, I crashed onto the cement floor. Terry walked behind me. I crawled away until I could get my shaking feet beneath me to stand.

"What are you doing?" Terry repeated as I looked in every cubby hole big enough to fit an adult woman.

"Janice?"

Terry put a hand to his head and stood to the side of the garage. "I don't understand why-"

"Where is she?" I wanted to poke Terry. Jam my index finger right in his chest and demand answers. An overwhelming surge of tenacity silenced my usual timidity.

Before Terry could answer, I spotted movement out of the side of my eye. From the garage window, a tarp rode the winter wind. Its tattered corner called to me.

"Did you hide her in there?"

"I don't know what you're talking about. Listen, you need to leave. Now! You do not know what you're walking into."

I slammed the garage door opener, next to the door to the kitchen, with my palm. It stuttered open, letting rainwater splatter the first two inches of the concrete floor. I slipped and slid across it as I hustled to the tarp. Terry followed me, slowly, like the villain of horror films. Like it didn't matter how fast I ran, he knew he was going to catch and silence me in the end. My raging imagination fed my adrenaline.

Wet vinyl tarps are hard to manage. Add in the wind, and I had to fight to loosen the covering. My active mind's eye had not prepared me for what was under the tarp—a white van.

My breath left me as if someone had punched me in the gut. I took a moment to ensure I hadn't been. But no, Terry stood howling at me from the opposite side of the van. He hadn't laid a hand on me, though he had plenty of opportunities.

I jerked open the door to the passenger side, surprised it was unlocked. I knew before looking, no one tied Janice up inside the van.

I called out to her anyway, "Janice?"

"I told you she's not here. She's at the hospital. With Dad." Terry's face fell. Was that sadness? Regret?

The wind tugged the tarp from my hand, and it fluttered into the Rockland's chain-link fence. Terry chased it.

I stood, leaving the door open, staring at the van. Its front fender was bent, but the damage looked older. Not from this morning. Someone recently repaired it, but the new paint job was shoddy. Chips cracked away, drawing one's eye to the indentation that had only partially been knocked back in place.

I walked to the back, holding my phone. This couldn't be the same van that Terry had us run down his mother. Was it? I scrolled for the picture I'd snapped some fourteen hours earlier. Sure, it was fuzzy, but it should be enough of a match to call the police. They could investigate further from there, and I could get out of town.

My text message from Scrubb interrupted my scrolling. I'd forgotten to acknowledge it earlier, and so every few minutes, it popped back up on the screen. I clicked on it in annoyance. Seven alphanumeric characters came into view. The same ones I stared at from the back of the van parked on the Rockland's property.

Terry strolled solemnly up to my right. I jumped.

"What is your deal? Seriously! My family has been through quite enough today!" Terry shouted over the wind and rain. Water streamed down his face. "How come you're always in the middle of things? Stirring up trouble?"

"Me?" I planted my hands on my hips. "I'm trying to save your mother!"

"Save my mother?" Terry laughed sarcastically. "Of course you are! That makes total sense."

"I know you have her," I said, though, at the moment, I had serious doubts. The van had thrown me for a loop. Still, I wasn't about to be swayed. I'd committed to a path, and I was plodding down it full steam ahead.

I invited myself back inside the Rocklands' home. Standing there, dripping on the kitchen tile, the details of the room soaked in. Drawers were tossed on the floor. Cabinet doors were flung wide open. Their contents were scattered everywhere. A tiny peek into the living room revealed a similar level of ransacking.

Terry stood in the doorway between the kitchen and the garage.

"You weren't hurting your mother?"

"Hurting my mom? No. What? Why would you think that?" he stammered.

"What were you looking for?"

"Me? Nothing. I came home to this mess. I've been trying to figure out if they took anything." Terry tossed the dripping tarp onto the garage floor.

He took two steps inside, and I took two steps back from him.

"*Was* anything taken?" I asked, suddenly weak in the knees. I was so confused. Was Terry just trying to lull me into a corner, or was he really as innocent as he pretended to be? I leaned against the back of a chair.

"Just the spare shop keys," he said. "Why would you think I'd hurt my mom?"

"You didn't?"

Terry choked on his words. "No. Never. Mom's-"

"What about your father? You're telling me you didn't try to drown him in a mop bucket earlier?"

Terry's face grew red. He waved his hands in the air in front of himself. "Why would I do that?" he asked. Growing louder, he added, "How would I do that? Why?"

"For your part of the will," I countered.

"The will? The will that split everything between Pearl and me? Why would I do that? I'm not sure if you noticed, but I kinda get a free ride around here. Sure, Dad's on the stingy side, but he's setting boundaries. Like any good dad." Terry pulled out the chair across from mine and plonked down into it. Exhaustion paled his usually dark complexion. "Geez, Penny. You're crazy!"

I'd been called worse. With my shoulders still hunched and ready to flee or fight, I took one long deep breath before I asked Terry, "Then if you're not trying to kill your mom and dad, who is? Where's your mother?"

Terry glanced at me as he responded, "I don't know who would want to kill them. Smack them around a bit, sure. But kill them. No way. Not that it's any of your business, but Mom's with Dad at the ER. Where else would she be?"

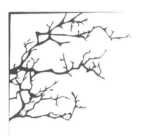

24

IT STUMPED ME. OF COURSE, Janice would be with Ken. Why had I thought otherwise? I should have gone to the hospital if I wanted to ensure Janice was safe. That wouldn't make sense, either. She would be safer there than she'd be anywhere else. At least if the worst happened, she'd have medical staff at the ready.

I rubbed the back of my neck. Embarrassed and still skeptical of Terry, I stared at him as his hair dripped onto the tablecloth.

If it wasn't Terry, who else could it have been? Surely, it wasn't Pearl, the discarded and blind step-sister. My words tumbled from my mouth without hindrance. "Why did you hire a P.I. to trail Pearl?"

"What?" Terry scoffed at me, but was too overwhelmed to avoid my prying. "How did you know about that? Not even Mom knows about that."

"I'm pretty sure she does. But that's not what I asked."

"Pearl is my sister. I wanted to get to know her better."

"Couldn't you have just asked your dad where she was? Send her a card or an email?" My nose tickled as my wet hair stuck to my face. I brushed it away with the cuff of my coat sleeve.

"It's not that easy. You don't just stroll up to someone you haven't seen in years and start talking. Not with *our* past." Terry inspected his palms as he spoke.

If I'd found my long-lost sister, that's exactly what I would've done. I would have run full speed up to her and wrapped her in a hug. I wouldn't tiptoe around and have strangers take pictures of her from a distance.

"You mean the accident?"

"How did you? Never mind, I don't want to know. I just want you out of my house and out of my life! Now!" He rose abruptly from his seat and took an intentional step of intimidation toward me.

"I know a lot. Like the fact that the van parked in your yard is the same one that blinded Pearl, and if my gut is right, it's the same one that tried to crush your mother."

Terry blinked. "There's no way. Don't you think the police would have discovered the van years ago? Like right after Pearl's accident?" He gestured with his hands in frustration. "It's not our van, anyway. It's only been in our yard for the last year."

"That doesn't mean it's not the same van. Look!" I showed Terry my text message from Scrubb and the photo of the van from the morning.

"You're cracked. If you're so convinced that the weapon that wrecked my family and nearly smashed my mother is that van." Terry pointed to the outside wall. "Then you're at the wrong house. Ask Jack! That's his old delivery van. It's parked here until Dad gets it fixed up. Then I'll take over the delivery route."

It was my turn to be overwhelmed. I felt my knees soften and wanted nothing more than to sit in a kitchen chair and have a good think.

Jack? What would Jack have to do with Pearl? Why would Jack run down Janice? For breaking up their pretend relationship? Or maybe it was only pretend to bystanders? Maybe it was a longtime romance, undercover?

I didn't get to mull it over any longer. Terry snagged my elbow and shoved me toward the front door. I dug my heels in and struggled to break his grasp. His frustration had made Terry much stronger than he looked. He had me in the foyer and reached for the knob with his free hand when his cell phone rang.

He answered without releasing me. Conversation on my end of the call was clipped. Terry put away his phone and released my elbow.

"Mom says the alarm system went off at the store. I've got to go check it out."

I ripped free from Terry. "How come vandals are messing with your house and the shop? Doesn't that strike you as weird?"

"No. It strikes me as none of your business. But You're in luck. I'll drive you back to your car, and then you can get out of my life."

He grabbed his jacket and nudged me back to the garage. I did not want to be stuck in a car with Terry. Especially in his current state. The tingling feeling that had prompted me to believe he was a very clumsy murderer had left. I wasn't certain what Terry was, exactly. But not for a moment was I going to assume he was safe.

Trucking at high speeds over potholes in the rain nearly had me heaving out the window. I squinted my eyes in concentration. There was a limited amount of time to talk with Terry and gather more intel.

"Why did you want to find Pearl? And why didn't you want your mother to know?"

Terry swallowed before he spoke. He was nervous and thrown off his center. I couldn't imagine him talking to me so freely otherwise. "Mom has been through a lot of things. Hard things. Things that have broken her. She's not the bubbly person you see at the store. Not all the time, anyway."

"Your dad is?" I asked. I couldn't fathom the flip in personality was as severe as Terry was hinting at.

He laughed. "Dad's the same soft-hearted tyrant everywhere he goes. He keeps people at arm's length, and all the while, he's figuring out ways to secretly gift them with something or other. A job. A van. A new life." He chuckled again; a steely coldness tainted the sound. "That's why he made mom hire you."

"I thought *she* wanted me?"

"Mom can't stand being around younger women. She says they remind her of Pearl and cause her too much pain. But really, she's vain and can't take the competition. That's why I couldn't tell her about Pearl. She'd freak out and think I was going to leave her."

"I'm not competition." I shuddered. It wasn't possible that Janice's friendliness with me had been a shell game. Or was it?

"No, you're not." Terry hurled the words like a javelin, hoping to hurt me. He skidded up to the front of the shop and tossed on the emergency brake. "You go around back. I'll go in the front."

He leaped from the car and ran to the door.

I jogged around back. How was I supposed to get in? I stood at the door, getting drenched. A racket next to the back dumpsters made me cringe. Spades came yowling from the alleyway and straight to me.

"Poor Ace of Spades," I cooed at him as I lifted him and sheltered him in my coat. I'd completely forgotten to call him back to the van before heading off to Terry.

I paced, waiting for Terry to let me in. In haste, I ran around the front. Remembering all the attacks of the day, it did not thrill me to dive into the dark shop and into who knows what. It didn't seem likely to be good for my health.

I couldn't hear anything or see anything from my tiny corner out front. I returned to the back. It was no good. The door was locked.

Spades wriggled inside my coat. I patted him through the heavy covering. Jingling sounds came from my pocket. I had the spare keys. No one stole them from the house. Terry had left them for me earlier that day.

Feeling like a raving moron, I held Spades with one hand and unlocked the door with the other. The door jerked away from me before I could get my bearings.

A tall man in a ski mask loomed over me for only a second before he shoved me into the kitchen of Rocky Grounds.

25

THE BACK LIGHTS WERE blaring compared to the storm-darkened outside world. Whirling from a coffee roaster created a rhythmic white noise in the background. It might have been a cozy atmosphere if they did not force me to stand with my hands linked behind my head next to the roaster.

Spades clawed into my belly to keep his balance, still hiding in my hoodie. Not to mention, Terry sat zip-tied to the center island, knocked out cold. Possibly chloroformed, since I didn't see a wound.

The masked man's partner peeped out of the office to check on the situation. Considerably shorter than the first man, this character seemed to make up for his lack of stature by growing more and more agitated. He'd search frantically, growled to himself, popped back into the kitchen, and then repeated the process.

After many rounds of such behavior, the short vandal rushed me and stuck a small blade to my throat.

"Where is it?"

I gulped. I knew that voice. My throat thickened along the blade. "Janice?"

Using her free hand, Janice pulled her mask back.

"What are you doing?" her cohort whispered. "The cameras." He motioned to the corners of the room.

Janice's scowl made my skin creep. Her partner, I was assuming to be Jack, reacted similarly. He took a step backward.

"What did I tell you? Don't you remember the plan? All of this is going, poof." Janice gestured to the stovetop.

Jack shrugged.

"Gas leak, remember?" Janice nodded towards the bound Terry. "Dumb butt, there, forgot to turn off the gas after coming in to fill a last-minute order. He left in a panic after receiving the phone call that his father had just died. From me, of course. At least that was the original idea."

I was happy to let them chat between themselves while I looked around for a weapon or a means of escape- until she mentioned Ken.

"Ken's dead?" I croaked.

Janice met my skeptical gaze with a look I'd never seen lurking behind her usually sunny disposition. It was malevolent, plotting, wicked. How had she covered this part of her for so long? Even in moments when there was no way she'd known I was watching, she never faltered.

The happy servant, wife, and friend were all masks for a conniving, patient, meticulous murderer. Her voice chilled me even deeper than her look.

"He died in my arms." She patted a mock tear from her cheek. "Poor Ken. Totally screwed up my plans. So now Terry'

"No, Janice, you didn't say Terry was part of this." Jack, still in his ski mask, whined. "Not again."

Again? I questioned. "Pearl?" I whispered, not meaning to let the name slip from my lips.

"What do you know about Pearl?" Jack whimpered, alarm thickening in his voice. "Janice, she knows about Pearl."

"Is that right, Penny? Why don't you tell us what you think you know?" Janice leaned against the counter, flicking the blade of her knife playfully against the cooling bowl of the largest coffee roaster.

26

WHAT WAS I SUPPOSED to say? What could I say that might save Janice and me from the Raven's plans? I hadn't seen my feathered friend land on Janice Rockland since the accident, but that didn't mean he'd changed his mind.

I wondered, "The accident? Both accidents? Pearl's and yours? They weren't, were they?"

"Weren't what? Accidents?" Janice grinned. "Geez, Penny, you're quicker than I pegged you. Of course, they weren't accidents. I needed Pearl out of the way, and I needed an alibi for Ken's death. All carefully planned. Until now. Thanks to you, I'm winging it."

"Janice?" Jack spoke with shaky dread, dripping from every word. He was terrified.

Maybe it wasn't a romantic relationship I'd been witnessing. Perhaps it was a long-lived case of friendly blackmail. But that would mean, "Jack, you're the one who ran down Pearl! Why?"

Jack's hand trembled. "Janice, I can't. I can't."

"Will you shut up, Jack! If you'd done as I'd said, we'd be clear. Now, I have to improvise. Instead of collecting all Ken's cash, we'll have to settle for what I've already skimmed from the accounts.

Terry would have kept his mouth shut for us, not kicking his sister out of her home. Though, honestly, the kid only lived with him for the first four years of his life. Why he'd want to take care of her now is beyond me."

Janice left my side and stormed over to her accomplice. She ripped the mask from his face and tossed it to the floor. I adjusted the angry cat in my hoodie and stopped his claws from tattooing through my shirt.

Jack's eyes radiated pure terror. He'd underestimated Janice. That was plain. Was that enough of a reality check to get Jack to stop in his tracks and decide to help me and Terry escape? I doubted it. But I could push him, just a little closer to the right choice.

"You know, Jack." I struggled for calm, but my voice wavered. "Janice has had you do all the dirty work. Pearl. Janice's accident... Did she have you drown Ken, too? What else have you done to keep her hands from getting dirty?"

Jack's eyes flickered. His trust in Janice was melting before my eyes. If the couple wasn't a pair of money-hungry homicidal maniacs, I might have cried. Their bond wasn't as strong as either of them had believed it to be. I took one more leap.

"What about your wife? Is she really missing? Or did Janice have you kill her, too? Silence her?"

It didn't surprise me. There was no telling how many of us were going to survive this situation.

On the floor, Terry stirred. He shook his head and coughed. Janice flinched but did not turn around. She placed a hand on each side of Jack's face, forcing him to look straight into her eyes.

Suddenly, Ken's song made sense. Janice couldn't hide anymore. Her lying ways were unweaving before her. She struggled to keep at least one of her men under her villainous thumb.

"Jack, you can't believe what Penny's saying. Honey, she's desperate. Can't you see that? She'd say anything to keep breathing. Any minute, she'll promise us she won't talk if we let her go. It's classic bartering. Don't fall for it."

Jack's eyes set firmly at Janice. "Like I fell for you? Over and over and over again. What have I done?"

Terry's voice echoed from the floor. "You've murdered my father and your wife. For a woman incapable of feeling."

Jack flinched as he digested Terry's words.

"She's about to have you help her kill her son," I said, backing Terry up.

"*Your* son," Terry said. Anger and sadness blended in his slurring speech.

Jack looked at Janice and back at Terry. If Terry was serious, Jack had a lot of drama to deal with on top of deciding whether to kill us all.

Janice frowned. She stepped away from Jack, dropping her arms to her side. "That's why I didn't invite you to the party, Terry. You never were bright enough to know when to keep your mouth shut."

Janice strolled calmly over to Terry, lifted her foot, and kicked her son in the ribs. Hard. The boy she seemed to cherish was only a pawn, just like the rest of us. Once his uses had run dry, there was nothing left linking the mother to the son. It was frightening.

Terry coughed and moaned. Being tied to the kitchen island stretched his husky body and exposed his tender spots all the more. The kick would've hurt badly enough without the added vulnerability.

I cradled Spades in my arms. He hid under my multiple layers. Backing toward the office, I hoped to get to a phone before Janice stopped belittling Terry.

Jack blocked me. He grabbed my shoulders but didn't hit me. Confusion still marred his devastated face. "Is he my son?" he asked. As if *I* knew.

I shrugged. Given the events of the evening, I wouldn't believe a word Janice said. And would strongly doubt any conversation I'd had with her in the past.

"Tell him, Mom!" Terry cried out after taking another kick to the stomach. "Tell him how you've used him this entire time. You should tell him about the security feeds you have kept of him doing your dirty work. The vandalisms. Dad's murder. Pearl's accident. Tell him!"

Janice smiled. "He already knows."

"Why else would you stick around?" I whispered. "Love? She doesn't love you. She doesn't know how to love."

Jack's face reddened. He shoved me to the floor. Using my hands to break my fall meant there was nothing to keep my coat closed. Spades leaped from my chest, mid-fall, and took off to the highest perch he could climb. He clawed his way up Jack's legs and straight to his face. Scratching as he went.

I hit the ground with a jolting thud, but didn't take the time to regain my breath. I crawled back toward the island, as far from Jack and my livid cat as possible. All while keeping my distance from Janice.

"Where are your stupid files?" she roared at Terry. "I'm tired of digging for them! You have them, I know that. I've seen the flash drive. Not smart of you to hide it in the office. But you and Ken weren't the smartest cookies in the jar."

When Terry looked at me, Janice kneeled and grabbed him by his widow's peak. She jerked his head back and glared down at him—full of venom and urgency.

"Someone stole them," Terry whimpered.

"Who, the vandals?" Janice snickered. "Haven't you added that up yet? We're the vandals." She pointed to her and Jack. "I took the box that I hid the files in earlier. It was empty. Then I found the envelope with the will copies, but no drive."

Terry's eyes tracked to me, even in his distressed state. I didn't have the drive. I'd left it in the envelope. Or had I?

I dug into the pockets of my coat, the same one I'd borrowed from the Rocklands. Sure enough, a hard rectangular shape met my fingertips.

Janice was still absorbed with Terry. However, Jack, having freed himself of Spades, saw me. Recognition rocked his expression.

"Penny has it!" he said, launching at me.

My angry cat snapped at him, causing him to stumble into the mop stand. I hurried away as Jack struggled to right himself for a second attempt to capture the USB.

"Why do I have to handle everything?" Janice hollered.

I scooted closer to Terry the moment Janice left him to handle Jack. Snatching a pair of kitchen shears, I cut through one of his zip ties.

I looked back to see Janice smack Jack on the back of the head with the bean scale. The clanking rattled my teeth as Jack plummeted. His bones crunched as his jaw hit the hard floor. The sound turned my stomach. His body came to rest at an angle too sharp to be healthy. If he wasn't dead, Jack was definitely dying.

Janice watched blood trickle out from Jack's hairline, and then she set her eyes on me.

27

TERRY JERKED AGAINST his last restraint in a frenetic flailing motion. It was his last resort to free himself before his cold-hearted mother turned her wrath toward him. After all, he had been the one to rock the boat and hire the private investigator.

"There's nothing on the drive!" Terry shouted. "Just pictures of Pearl and dad."

Janice narrowed her eyes. "Don't taunt me. I know what's on the drive—an entire folder of encrypted information. Something tells me you weren't clever enough to open it. Neither was your father. So my secrets end with you."

Again, Janice rolled up to Terry's left and kicked him. This time in the head, knocking him silly. His eyes didn't close, but they weren't aware either. Terry was semi-unconscious and still tied to the island. He lulled in his in-between state.

Janice flipped on all four burners on the stovetop. Pulling her hair away, she blew out their flames. "Poor Penny," she said. "Wrong place at the wrong time. Be sure to thank Ken for hiring you when you see him."

Spades yowled and retreated up the mop handle and to the soap rack, away from all the pesky humans. I was glad he was out of the way.

Janice bent over in front of me and reached her good hand out to grab mine.

At the exact moment, the roaster finished its program and expelled beans into the cooling bowl. Steaming and smoking inside their metal dish, I took the beans, bowl and all, and chucked it at Janice's face.

Most of the beans bounced away. A few stuck to her skin, branding the flesh around her eyes. Some cascaded down her shirt and burrowed deeper into her underbelly. She yowled and writhed, trying to escape their searing freshness.

I took my opportunity to stand. With a force I didn't know I had, I lifted the security monitor, ripped it free of its cords, and chucked it at the flailing Janice.

The small screen hit my boss in the chest and forced her to the ground. She was stunned but not knocked cold. I jerked my phone from my pocket and dialed emergency. Then I hustled to the stovetop. The smell of gas was already overwhelming the scent of coffee in the small kitchen.

I turned off two of the four burners before Janice tugged me back by the neck of my coat. She jerked me an arm's length from the stovetop before I slithered out of the unfastened sweater, taking a red stove knob with me.

The force of my escape brought me to my knees on the hard floor. Thankfully, it also threw Janice for a literal loop. She slid across the ground, tumbling over her one-time boy toy.

I doubted if she'd ever loved him. It was like Terry said; Janice probably loved no one. Not really.

I turned back in time to see Janice struggling to regain her balance. Her sensible shoes slipped in the slick and growing puddle of Jack's blood. Then, from on top of the soap rack, Spades hurled himself at Janice. He bounced off her head and landed in collected cat coolness on the kitchen island.

Janice teetered and swayed before her legs shot out from under her. She landed with a crack louder than Jack's fall had echoed. Face down in the soapy mop bucket.

I crawled to Terry. The gas fumes were becoming overwhelming. I cut the last tie that held him to the island. He was still half knocked out.

Locking my wrists under his armpits, I flexed every muscle I had in my back, biceps, and buns to drag the man from the kitchen.

Jack's, and Janice's bodies blocked the back entrance. There was no way I could lift Terry over them. I began the long trudge to the front.

The remains of the last bout of vandalism made the journey all the harder. There was a small path cleared, but it didn't stop Terry's legs from snagging on every protruding item or upturned sales rack.

"Spades," I called, coughing. "Come on, you amazing cat!"

I don't know why I bothered to call him. Spades typically ignored me whenever I spoke his name. Plus, he was still mad at me for ditching him to hunt a killer.

Still, by the time I reached the front door, he was at my side. He sat on Terry's stomach, licking himself. As if dragging a body was a task he supervised every day.

Leaning on the front door, I took a long suck of air, using my damp shirt as a face mask. I shoved with all my strength. There wasn't much of it left. Dizziness overwhelmed me.

"C'mon," I hollered at no one.

I wasn't sure there was a God. But T.C. talked about him constantly. It was the only thing, other than my inexplicable attraction to him, that made goosebumps skip along my skin whenever we chatted. Scrubb and T.C. had both said they were praying for me. Specifically.

Even if I didn't take encouragement from who they were praying to, their good wishes and thoughts could strengthen me. Right?

"Please," I whispered through gritted teeth as I summoned everything I had to pull myself, my cat, and Terry through the front door.

We landed in a pile just outside Rocky Grounds. The rain washed away the sweat of pulling Terry, but not the massive headache forming behind my eyes.

I turned Terry onto his side. Spades hid from the downpour beneath the young man's arm.

Taking cleansing petrichor breaths, I debated with myself. If Janice was still alive, I had to help her out of the shop. I did not know how long it had taken me to rescue Terry. There was no way to know unless I went back inside.

I tucked the flash drive into the back pocket of Terry's jeans. If I didn't make it out or if Janice was merely lying in wait, I didn't want the evidence against her to slip away.

I staggered to standing and took one last breath. As I charged ahead, back into the gift shop, a pair of powerful arms wrapped around me.

"You don't wanna do that, Hun." It was Betty Fae. "Help is here. Let them do their job. From what I saw, you've done more than your share."

The gruff and large woman did not release me. She flipped me to face her and enveloped me in an enormous hug. I fell apart. Crying and shaking. Betty Fae held me all the tighter.

"It's the adrenaline," she whispered. "Let it all out."

She stroked my hair as I wept on her shoulder. Firefighters raced past me and into Rocky Grounds.

"Gas," I explained. "The stove."

One entered to shut off the stove and open the doors. He was standing beside Betty Fae and me moments later.

"We've got two dead inside," he said.

"From the gas?" another man asked.

Firefighter one shook his head. Betty Fae pulled me closer, wrapping her massive raincoat over my shoulders.

Spades circled my ankles, checking on me like he often did. For a wild cat, he was unusually intuitive and compassionate but never liked to admit it. Like me in cat form.

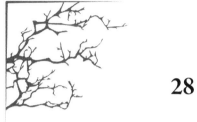

28

TWO DAYS LATER, THE cops cleared me to leave town. Terry met me at the shop with my last paycheck.

He wasn't quite himself yet. I wasn't sure he'd ever go back to his normal self. That wasn't necessarily a bad thing. Not if normal Terry was the lazy man with the lingering eyes, I'd previously encountered.

"I don't know what I'm going to do, yet," Terry said, as he shuffled his feet when I'd asked him about the future. "I think I'm going to let Pearl decide, especially now that she knows she's my stepsister and not blood-related. If she wants to keep the store open and help me run it, then we'll make that happen. If she'd rather wash her hands of it and live off Dad's money, we can do that too. Either way is fine with me."

"Won't it be weird? Sticking around after what happened?"

Terry laughed. "Not as weird as it was before." He snorted and shoved away a stray tear with the back of his hand. "You didn't know Mom. Not really. She had an unflappable game face. Even got me believing it from time to time. Dad suspected Mom had something to do with Pearl's accident. At least, he often alluded to his suspicions when the two of us were alone and drinking. But I figured he was just bitter. Until I hired that private investigator."

I crossed my arms and leaned against the front door of Rocky Grounds. "Why did you hire him?"

Growing agitated with my presence and not at all hiding the fact, Terry grimaced and grunted. "Honestly? Mom put me up to it. She thought Dad was seeing lawyers. Getting ready to leave us. I told her she was nuts. But she insisted. So, I hired him on the sly. Now, I see she didn't want to get her hands dirty. What she didn't know was that Dad had been visiting Pearl, not a lawyer. When she stumbled across my reports from the investigator, she went nuts."

I wondered if Terry had been dumb enough to hide his files in the store safe, where his mother was bound to find them. Or had Janice found them beforehand and then smuggled them to the one place she knew her men would never look: work.

What I really wanted to know was, "What were the encrypted files on the flash drive? The ones your mom was so certain proved her guilt?"

Terry snickered to himself. "I don't have a clue." He scratched his head. "I know less about computers than mom did. She was right. I couldn't open them."

I felt the look of judgment carve my eyebrows into a V and tried to fight it. But seriously, if Janice had realized Terry had literally nothing to blame her for Pearl's accident and Ken's murder, would she have gone so ballistic? Or would she have quietly slipped out of town with Jack? I guess we'd never know.

The police would definitely open the file. It didn't matter. The truth had already done its damage, as had the Raven.

Terry frowned at me and shuffled his feet.

This was the usual posture I recognized as the brush-off. If I didn't depart soon, anger would replace stoic patience.

"Well, good luck," I said.

"Yeah, sure," Terry mumbled. "You too."

That was it. I was free to move along.

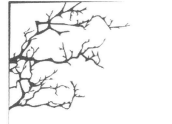

29

MILES AWAY FROM ROCKY Grounds, I pulled my van over to a strip mall outside of a medium-sized town. Strip malls were the perfect place to find weird and desperate employers without picky paperwork standards. That wasn't why I was there.

It was late, and I was a little lost. I took out my old school road atlas. GPS and Wi-Fi worked great in towns or cities, but back roads required written maps.

I put a small gold flag on the town. I'd revisit it someday if I needed work. But that wasn't what was on my mind.

A safe place to park for the night and dinner was.

A thrift shop on the edge of the parking lot called to me. I entered the warmth of the shop and meandered toward the gadget aisle. My eyes landed on my quarry just as my phone rang.

There were only two people who would call me. With my weekly check-in with Joe coming tomorrow afternoon, I doubted it was him.

"Hello," I said, pinching the phone between my shoulder and ear.

"Just had to make sure you were alive." T.C.'s voice trembled.

Was he nervous to talk to me? I shivered. It wasn't unlike me to imagine his concern. One could only live alone for so long before they started dreaming up relationships where there weren't any.

"I texted and emailed," I said, forcing coolness to my tone.

T.C. continued as I paid my purchase at the counter. "I know. I just needed to hear it for myself, I suppose. How did your meeting with Terry go?"

I explained the awkward exchange on my journey back to Godzilla. Spades sat in the driver's seat, glaring at me as I approached.

"At least you got your last check. I was worried he'd back out of paying you without his father there to make him."

T.C. wasn't far off. "He docked my pay for the use of the electricity. But that's no biggie. What annoyed me was the chunk he took out of my check for my morning coffees."

"He didn't!"

I slid into my van, petting Spades after I shut and locked the door. "He did. Four dollars for every single day I worked."

"Petty," T.C. said. "He must not understand that you saved his life."

"Ha!" I said, bitterly pulling my curtains closed. "Ruined his life. Is more like it."

"That's not how I see it. I think your stay at Rocky Grounds was a resounding success."

I shook my head. "Everyone died. Ken, Jack, and Janice. Everyone the Raven marked. Dead. That's the opposite of success."

"Without the Raven, you wouldn't have been on the lookout. You wouldn't have been there to pull Terry out of the shop before he asphyxiated, or it went up in flames."

I agreed, despite myself. He had a point, though not an overwhelming tip in the scales. My "gift" was still a curse without end. But I could confess, if only to myself, there was a glimmer of light beyond its shadows. One day it would be nice to see the good, face to face, if there really was any there to see. That day would be a long time coming.

"I guess," was all I said to T.C.

"That's how I choose to see it," he said, fixed and firm in his blind trust in me and my ability. "Then again, I'm just the strange man with a weird podcast."

I giggled. T.C. was indeed a strange man. As much as I hated to admit it, it was nice having him on the other line. Cozy. Safe. Ish.

AFTER HE SIGNED OFF, I pulled on my favorite PJs and unfolded my bed. Spades, in a forgiving mood, curled on my feet. He purred as I listened to T.C.'s podcast, fast-forwarding through my answers and focusing only on his voice.

I laid back on my pillow, my eyes blinking in weariness, and stared at my new second-hand air popper. Tonight, I'd sleep in a well-lit parking lot. Tomorrow morning, I was roasting myself fresh coffee beans.

And then? Who knew?

The Extra Extra
Ordinary Podcast

T.C: HELLO AND WELCOME to the Extra Extra Ordinary Podcast. The podcast that dives into the semi paranormal events of everyday life. This is episode 77.

I'm T.C. In the studio today with my producer, Scrubb. Say Hey Scrubb.

Scrubb: Hey.

T.C.: All our AbiNormals out there recognize this week's sponsor. Once again, we're brought to you by the Heliotrope Experimental Community. Building the future before your very eyes. More on Heliotrope later in the podcast.

It's not often in Extra Extra life that we get to follow up, in person, to a reader testimony. Let alone have the subject of the letter agree to join us live.

Scrubb: Mostly because Bigfoot hates interviews.

T.C.: Today, we're beyond blessed to have the Small Town Seer Girl on the phone with us. For those of you who might be in the dark, Seer Girl has graced three separate listener emails in the last year. Scrubb, will you give us a quick rundown of the most exciting account? Changing the names to protect the innocent... of course.

Scrubb: Sure thing.

Dennis from Dairyland writes:

T.C. and Scrubb,

The night of the party, everything was cool. Just a bunch of us hanging out at my friend's cabin, drinking and listening to music. A guy from town thought it would be nice to invite the new employee from the local greasy spoon to hang out.

She seemed normal enough. The party went on—nothing out of the ordinary.

Until close to one a.m, I was out back, near the hot tub, when the screaming started inside the cabin.

The new girl was going berserk. She was busting into every room, yelling for people to get out of the cabin and head toward the lake.

We all thought she was crazy. Or maybe she'd had a little too much to drink. After all, everything was normal.

My girlfriend confronted her. She asked the girl what was wrong. She said there was a fire, and we needed to run to the lake before the cabin burned down.

I hurried inside and helped my friend check the cabin. No smoke. No fire. No nothing. Still, the new girl insisted we were all in danger. She even forced my girlfriend to drive her back to town.

Less than an hour later, while my girlfriend was still gone, some guy thought it would be fun to make brownies. One thing led to another, and before the brownies were done baking, the kitchen went up in flames.

My friend and I tried to put it out, but all the fire extinguishers were dead. The fire was relentless. The entire property was ablaze in minutes. We had no choice but to flee the cabin.

Everyone got out of the house, alive. Though a few people were hurt. We stood along the edge of the lake, watching my friend's cabin burn to the ground and waiting for the fire department.

My girlfriend made it back in time to see me loaded into an ambulance. She told me the girl didn't stop warning her about the fire and begged her not to let anyone cook in the cabin. She'd asked her to call me, but my girlfriend had thought the girl was nuts.

We all did.

Now, we know better.

We're still not sure how she knew about the fire. Unless she tampered with the stove before she left, I guess we'll never be sure. Though listening to your podcast has proved trouble follows this chick around.

One thing is for sure, if we ever meet again, I'm running the other way. Thanks for sharing my story. - Dennis

T.C.: Thanks Dennis, for writing to us. Today we have Seer Girl on the phone. She's mentioned by name in our letters. For brevity's sake and to keep her identity private, we're calling her Sierra.

Hello Sierra, it's great to have you on the podcast.

Penny: Hello. I'm glad to be here. I guess.

T.C.: Do you mind if we get right to our questions? There are quite a few listeners intrigued by your story. Or at least the stories about you?

Penny: I'll answer the best I can. Though I'm not sure I know more than Dennis does.

T.C.: Do you remember the event Dennis mentions in his letter?

Penny: It would be hard to forget.

T.C.: Without throwing blame, does Dennis have his facts straight?

Penny: I don't know what happened after I left. Mostly, he's got it right.

T.C.: That means you saw the fire coming?

Penny: Not exactly.

Scrubb: What do you mean, not exactly?

Penny: Not exactly.

T.C.: We have various sources claiming that you see the future. That you accurately predict events before they've happened.

Penny: I don't know what your sources say. But I don't see the future.

T.C.: You do sense or see something that leads you to believe something is going to happen?

Penny: I guess you could say that.

T.C: Did you know the fire was going to break out?

Penny: I knew it was a very strong possibility.

T.C.: Did you know it would take place in the kitchen?

Penny: I guessed it would.

Scrubb: Can you explain that night to us?

Penny: I'll do my best.

I went to the cabin with a guy from work. He hadn't given me much choice. I thought he was driving me home, but he took me there. There was a party going on. It wasn't rowdy, but it was crowded.

My "friend" ditched me shortly after we arrived. He ran off with another girl. Which meant I was on my own with a bunch of strangers—people I'd seen around town but didn't know.

I helped myself to a room in the back of the cabin. — an office. There, I borrowed a book and started reading.

In a few hours, a couple burst into the room. I guess they thought it was empty. They announced pizza had arrived. I went and grabbed a slice. Someone knocked into me and spilled their root beer all over one of the beige couches. I tried to clean it up. And that's when I saw it.

T.C.: Saw what? A fire

Penny: No. A shape in the stain.

T.C.: What kind of shape?

Penny: A bear in a hat.

Scrubb: Like Smokey the Bear? The mascot of preventing forest fires?

Penny: Exactly! That's what I thought. But I wasn't sure. I can't go by the glimpses alone.

T.C.: Glimpses?

Penny: That's what I call them. Glimpses. Sneak peeks into the future.

T.C.: So you *can* see the future.

Penny: Not really. I just get these little clues. I have to add things up for myself.

T.C.: Do bears mean fire?

Penny: No. I've seen animals before. Sometimes they mean a literal animal attack.

T.C.: Which animal do you see most often?

Penny: A Raven.

T.C.: What does a raven mean?

Penny: Death. Usually murder. But always death. I have to gather context clues from what's happening around me.

T.C.: What context clues told you a fire was coming?

Penny: Well, besides the bear, there was the radio. It shut off in the middle of a rap song and Johnny Cash played.

Scrubb: Let me guess. Good old, Ring of Fire?

Penny: Right! Pretty obvious! Then the surrounding people started complaining about how dry the summer had been and how one match could light the woods up. In fact, one girl was cursing at her boyfriend for smoking outside. That added up to fire to me.

T.C.: Did you warn people immediately?

Penny: No. I should have. I'm never sure my glimpses are correct or if I'm interpreting them correctly. Believe it or not, I don't like being pegged as the crazy new girl.

I waited a bit. Checked the house. Looked for signs of danger. And more and more glimpses kept popping up. Until I couldn't keep silent, that's when I started warning people.

Many of whom couldn't be bothered to stop making out long enough to listen. When no one cared, which is pretty typical, I begged for a ride home.

T.C.: Your driver mentioned that's when you warned her about the kitchen. How did you know the fire would start there?

Penny: I didn't. But Hank Williams interrupted her pop station with Hey Good Lookin'. I figured it was a safe bet.

T.C.: Does it make you feel any better to hear that you were right?

Penny: No. Not one bit. People got hurt. I should have stopped them. I didn't.

Scrubb: One of the most injured was your friend. The guy who brought you to the party only to ditch you. Doesn't that seem very coincidental?

Penny: That's what the entire town said. I had people show up at work and spit at me the next day.

Scrubb: Is that typically what happens when one of your "glimpses" ends in trouble?

Penny: They all end in trouble. And yes, it's pretty standard. It took less than a week for me to lose my job and any friends I had in town. Then I drove off to a new place.

T.C.: Why bother telling your story to them? If things end so poorly for you?

Penny: I don't want anyone getting hurt. Ever.

T.C.: That's fair. But why publicize it? Even to our smallish audience? Why tell us?

Penny: Have you ever had a secret so terrible it was physically heavy? I'm tired of carrying it alone.

T.C.: We're glad you've chosen to share it with us.

Scrubb: Are you willing to dive deeper into your glimpses? Maybe on another call?

Penny: If you think it would help anyone.

T.C.: Maybe we could help *you*.

Scrubb: Thanks, Sierra. Unfortunately, T.C., our time is up for this episode.

T.C.: There's never enough time. Don't forget my AbiNormals, to check out what they're planning at Heliotrope Experimental Community. Why wait when you can enjoy the future today?

Thanks, Sierra, for joining us. We look forward to our next chat.

If you have questions for Sierra or have a semi-paranormal story to share, click the link in the description and send it our way.

Remember, there is no normal. Embrace the Extra Extra Ordinary. See you next time.

Free Ebook- Penny Mystery 1.5[1]

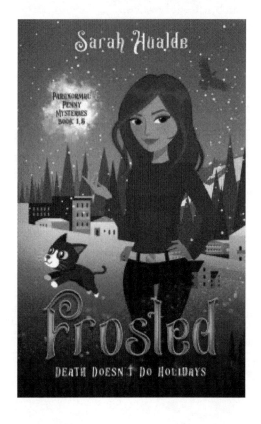

Supernatural Suspense meets Paranormal Mystery in the Penny Nicols Series. You'll cheer for the Paranormal Penny, her quirky cat, and their extra extraordinary friends.

Don't stop at Grounded. See what the winter holds for Penny. Download Frosted- Penny's seasonal short.
For FREE on Ebook
Visit the site below to snag your copy:
https://storyoriginapp.com/giveaways/be376e58-a177-11ec-9c75-036090dfe8b2

;) enjoy

Did you love *Grounded*? Then you should read *Crushed*[2] by Sarah Hualde!

Making new friends can be terrifying.

Especially when your secret can kill them.

Working at a gym was never a dream for Penny.

But when the job lands in her lap, she grabs it with gratitude- until a random theft sets off a chain reaction orchestrated by the Raven.

Penny struggles to keep her friends safe as the clock ticks down.

She reaches out for support to defeat the darkness.

---

2. https://books2read.com/u/bxjxwJ

3. https://books2read.com/u/bxjxwJ

Can the paranormal podcasters help her take down Death? Or will Penny's secret claim another victim?

One thing is for sure; The Raven is up to his old tricks.

★Jump into the second Paranormal Penny Mystery and hang on tight.★

This fast-paced series will captivate you from start to finish. Read more at www.sarahhualde.com.

Also by Sarah Hualde

Honey Pot Mysteries
Missing on Main Street
Lethal in Lavender
Farmers Market Fatality
Death by Donation
Killer Con Fuego
Write and Wronged
Honey Pot Mystery Box Set 1

Paranormal Penny Mysteries
Grounded
Frosted
Crushed
Tailed
Cracked
Played

Standalone

Diary of a Dyslexic Homeschooler

Watch for more at www.sarahhualde.com.

About the Author

Sarah lives in California, in a home that brings her happiness and hay fever. She loves God, loves her family, and loves freshly brewed coffee. She has a husband who cooks, a son who stop animates, a daughter who loves animals, a dog that follows her everywhere, and a turtle who scowls at her condescendingly.

Her mother raised her on Mary Higgins Clark, Dianne Mott Davidson, and Remington Steele. Her grandmother shared True Crime stories with her as they plotted how to get away with the perfect murder. It's no surprise Sarah became a spinner of suspenseful tales brimming with quirky characters. Mysteries are in her blood. Not that she could survive one of her own stories.

She confesses, "I'd be snuffed out by Chapter two."

Join Sarah's Super Sleuth Squad and follow her on YouTube for behind-the-scenes insider info.

Super Squad Newsletter ---->
https://landing.mailerlite.com/webforms/landing/g1k6r0

YouTube-----> https://www.youtube.com/channel/
UCK9ywmqk_2k-mEssZMkEvBQ

Read more at www.sarahhualde.com.

Made in the USA
Monee, IL
25 March 2024

55779198R10099